THE FEUD

It was bad enough that the squatter named Jake had homesteaded in the middle of Sam Croft's calving ground, land he hadn't owned but which he had used for thirty years. But it was worse when Jake courted and married old Sam's daughter, Susan. Although he had disowned his daughter, when it came to her death Croft wanted his grandchildren. Susan's dying words were for Jake to take the children and flee. Jake tries, but could he manage to escape?

LEW GRAHAM

THE FEUD

Complete and Unabridged

LINFORD
Leicester

First published in Great Britain in 1994 by
Robert Hale Limited
London

First Linford Edition
published December 1995
by arrangement with
Robert Hale Limited
London

British Library CIP Data

Graham, Lew
The feud.—Large print ed.—
Linford western library
I. Title II. Series
823.914 [F]

ISBN 0–7089–7768–5

Published by
F. A. Thorpe (Publishing) Ltd.
Anstey, Leicestershire

Set by Words & Graphics Ltd.
Anstey, Leicestershire
Printed and bound in Great Britain by
T. J. Press (Padstow) Ltd., Padstow, Cornwall

This book is printed on acid-free paper

1

The Departure

SUNSHINE filtered through the yellowed curtains of the small bedroom. There was a faint breeze, which gave an impression of dancing lights playing their last game before sundown, pausing occasionally to touch the face of the woman lying on the bed.

Even through the transparency, the lines of pain, her face still had a quality of beauty that touched the soul of the man sitting by her side.

The woman opened her eyes and focused on her surroundings. She saw her husband and gently smiled. Her husband spoke quietly. "Susan, is there anything you want? More water?"

Susan noticed the furrows in the tanned face of her husband. She saw both the strength and gentleness that had caused her to fall in love with him. She raised her hand to his face then let it drop into his hand. Her eyes, faded blue, searched his face, she asked in a whispery voice where the children were.

His answer was slow. "Joseph is at the barn doing the chores, Sarah is gatherin' the eggs. They have the younger ones with them . . . Would you like to see them?"

Susan seemed not to have heard him. After a lengthy silence she spoke in a stronger voice. "Jake. You must load the wagon and get the children ready to leave."

He squeezed her hand. "There's time, Susan."

Her eyes briefly brightened. "No, Jake. You've got to leave tonight. You know they'll take the children away from you. We agreed . . . You promised you'd keep them with you." Her breathing increased. "My father will take them. I know, he owns most

2

of the valley and could do a lot for them, that's not what we want . . . You promised, Jake."

He soothed her gently. There were tears in her eyes. "I'll never let it happen, Susan."

"You'll leave . . . tonight?"

"We'll leave. Save your strength, Susan."

"There's not enough time, Jake. I want to say a little more. I love you very much, Jake . . . I've been very happy, more than you'll ever know. I feel a terrible sadness leaving you to care for the children . . . I was born on the ranch; I'd like to be buried here."

His voice was unsteady when he asked again if she'd like to see the children. She had exhausted all her strength. When she replied her voice was fading. "No. I'd rather they remembered me as I was, not as I am now."

Silence settled between them but their eyes met and held. They both thought of other times, happy times.

There was a longing to relive those times that was heart-wrenching.

Susan sighed. The sunlight was rapidly fading. She whispered softly, "Jake, promise me."

"I promise, Susan. We'll leave tonight."

The silence returned, bittersweet, agonisingly painful. Susan lay still in the bed. Tears filled Jake's eyes as he folded her hands, bent forward to kiss her cheek and her forehead. She looked as though she were sleeping.

He arose, stood looking at her and could not control his emotions, slid to the floor and wept at the bedside burying his face in a blanket. A small tapping at the door went temporarily unnoticed. When he arose moments later he recognised the deepening shadows. He lighted a candle on the little bedside table, pulled the sheet over her head, hesitated briefly before squaring his shoulders and going to the door.

As he closed the door behind himself

he saw four sombre faces looking up at him. He bent down and opened his arms. All four children fell into them and began crying.

As Jake arose, the youngest child was tugging at his sleeve. "Daddy. Daddy. Me 'ungry." Jake wiped his eyes on a sleeve, and asked Sarah, the eldest girl who was eight to see what she could find for the children to eat. Joseph, the oldest boy went to set bowls on the table, Sarah poured milk into tin cups, William, just turned five, put a biscuit beside each bowl, as their father lifted Lottie, who would be four in three months, onto a chair. Jake had been thankful Lottie was a quiet child, not into everything the way William had been at her age.

Jake sat at the table with them but ate nothing. They glanced at him. When they had eaten Jake looked solemnly at each child. He said, "We've got some hard work ahead. We'll load the wagon, take what's necessary an' leave the rest behind.

We got to do all this as fast as we can."

They regarded him solemnly. Sarah ventured a question. "Can Lottie take her dolly?"

Jake answered shortly. "Each of you can take your favourite things, but we've got to get going."

Sarah spoke for herself with tears in her eyes. "Can I take something of Mama's too?"

She favoured her mother, the same eyes, the features, hair and build. "Yes, each of you can take something of Mama's." He fought down the ache in his chest as he rose from the table. "Now let's get busy."

It would keep their minds off their mother. It would also give Jake a reason for activity, but his mind only left his memories when the children had questions.

They worked steadily into the dusk. They loaded the wagon with food, quilts, clothing, water, cooking utensils. Although it was late August and still very warm, where they were going into the highlands it would be cold at night. Jake had been preparing for this for some time. He had made a tarpaulin cover for the wagon. It would offer some protection from both the lowland heat and the high-country cold.

After the loading had been completed Jake went through the house room by room. He stopped in front of the closed door, settled himself for the last good-bye. He told the body under the sheet he was sorry he wouldn't be there to give Susan a proper burial, but this is the way they had planned it in order for Jake and the children to get a decent head-start in case her father came after him. His last words were: "I love you, Susan. I'll watch over the children as best I can."

He fought down his grief blew out the candle and walked quickly out of the room. As he paused near the fireplace to take down his rifle from its pegs he forced himself to think ahead.

He took a box of cartridges from a shelf and walked out the door.

The children were sitting in the wagon as solemn and silent as owls. He knew they would cry if he hesitated; this was the only home they had known and they were leaving their mother behind.

He pulled himself up into the wagon. "Ready?" he asked.

The three oldest ones answered almost in unison, "Yes, Pa." Lottie nodded her head and yawned at the same time.

The team of big, stout horses had no trouble with the loaded wagon. Jake took a back road that skirted the town that lay at the foot of the mountains. He had to put as many miles as possible between Sam Croft and the wagon as he could before Susan's father found she was dead, no simple task; wagons were slow, loaded or unloaded.

Lottie went to sleep in Sarah's lap. Jake told the boys to crawl into the back of the wagon and sleep because tomorrow there would be hard work to do.

He was thankful he had so many things to worry about; they did not ameliorate the ache in his chest but they kept his mind busy and diverted.

When daylight returned they stopped only long enough to rest and care for the team, gather wood for a breakfast fire, eat jerky and left-over biscuits and wash it all down with spring water.

When the trail got rougher Jake told the boys they could walk beside the wagon. They had been restless. Sarah sat in back of the wagon watching Lottie play with her doll. Neither girl seemed to particularly mind the jolting.

The sun was almost directly overhead when Jake stopped near a creek to rest the horses. There was graze but it was scanty, they were in timbered country.

When they had eaten the effect of the afternoon sun made them all drowsy.

Jake spread a blanket under a medium-sized tree and told them they could sleep for a few hours.

He slept too; he knew for a fact he'd have to drive the wagon again all night.

2

An Unexpected Shock

DOCTOR SUTHERLIN said Susan was doing poorly when he stopped by. He said we should go see her. I could be of some help with the children . . . Sam?"

Sam Croft's answer was curt. "No!"

"Even if she needs us?"

Sam's expression did not change. She pleaded with him. "At least send one of the riders over."

"Anna, that'd be the same as if I went myself." Sam went to the door where he paused to say, "I'll be back before dark."

Anna went to the window and watched him ride away. Sam Croft was a proud man. Too proud. During all the years they had been married she had never once gone against his wishes, but now the time had come. He was dead wrong; and regardless of the consequences, Anna's mind was made up. She tidied up the kitchen, threw some things she thought their daughter might need into a basket and went to the barn where she found one of the riders mending harness.

She hadn't wanted anyone to know where she was going, but quickly decided it might be better to have the rider accompany her in the event she had to stay with Susan. If she had to stay she could send word back by the rider, whose name was Lynch Miller.

She asked him to saddle two horses and accompany her to her daughter's place. Lynch looked surprised but all he said was, "Yes'm. You wait in the shade on the porch. I'll bring 'em over there."

Anna thanked him and returned to the porch. She could guess what Lynch was thinking; what her husband would say to him if he found out Lynch had accompanied his wife to see their daughter.

Anna Croft was a woman in her mid-forties, still attractive. Having had to suffer domination by Sam Croft, Lynch wondered if now she was being defiant, and while he liked Anna he did not like the position she had put him in by riding with her to the homestead; there was an excellent chance Sam would fire him.

He didn't want to be around when, or if, her husband found out about their ride together to see Susan. Knowing Sam; there was bound to be fireworks.

A flat blue-jay flew across the trail in front of them, scolding as it landed in a nearby tree, startling Anna out of deep thought.

She stopped to watch the bird as it continued to scold, scanned the surrounding area and could hardly believe they had already reached timberline.

Beautiful tall trees that stretched from where the land had been cleared to the

13

mountains and beyond. It was cooler now with only two more miles to go. Surely nothing could be wrong on such a beautiful day as this. She urged her horse to a faster pace until they reached the outskirts of the homestead's clearing.

Lynch felt Anna stiffen when they rode up to the front of the cabin.

"Something's wrong Lynch. I can feel it." She had a worried look on her face.

Lynch felt it too. For one thing it was too quiet. He told her to stay where she was and he'd have a look around the barn. Maybe they had all ridden into town for supplies, but he couldn't shake the feeling of foreboding.

After having a look around, Lynch rode back to the house. Not seeing Anna outside, he went into the house and found her sitting rocking softly in the chair by the bed. He froze when he saw Susan's body.

He turned to look at Anna. She wasn't crying.

He walked over and laid his hands on her shoulders, trying to make her look at him, but her gaze seemed to go right through him. He could have kicked himself for not checking the house first.

Well, it was too late for that now, he had to get her out of there.

"Come on, Missus Croft, let's get back to the ranch. I'll have a wagon sent over and see to things," he said as he tried to pull her gently to her feet. She jerked back shaking her head.

"No. I want to stay here with Susan for a while."

Lynch could understand that so he conceded for the time being.

"Doesn't she look at peace, Lynch?"

"Yes ma'm."

They lingered there a while longer with Lynch becoming increasingly uncomfortable. He thought even if Anna would cry, show some emotion, he could handle it better than just sitting in the unearthly quiet.

Lynch decided to try again. "At least

let's go into the other room and we can talk if you'd like." He laid his hand upon hers and added, "Ma'm?"

She reluctantly gave in, half leaning on him for support. He sat her down at the table and sat down across from her.

"You really should have a good cry, Missus Croft. Much better than holdin' it inside."

"I can't right now, Lynch. I'm too full of hate."

"Hate?" Lynch looked dumbfounded.

"I don't know exactly who my hate is directed at . . . Jake . . . for not sending for me? Or Sam, for being so stubborn, refusing to let me see my daughter and grandchildren. It's a mother's and grandmother's right to visit and share talks and laughter. And now it won't ever happen."

She leaned across the table, her lips quivering, "Do you have any idea how I felt having to sneak here when it should have been my right to come openly?"

16

She was waiting for some kind of answer, but he couldn't give her one, so instead he said, "I really think we should be getting back. We need to send someone to take care of things before very long." He couldn't very well come right out and say summer heat would make things unpleasant.

Lynch watched her face as he tried to figure what else he could do or say to get Anna out of the house, but she surprised him by abruptly arising and walking briskly past him out the door.

It was much warmer on the way back. Neither spoke but Lynch kept his eyes on Anna and when he noticed her swaying, stopped the horses and made her get off to rest.

No sooner did she touch ground, she became sick. She retched off and on for about half an hour, clinging to his arm as if it were the only thing in the whole world she could hang on to. His shirtsleeves was soaked from her sobbing.

Finally, her whole body seemingly

17

spent, he sat her down under a tree leaning her back against it, untied the bandana from around his neck dowsing it with water from his canteen, then gently but thoroughly applied it to her face and neck.

She looked up at him with a half smile as she said, "I bet I really look a mess."

"Missus Croft, from what you've been through, you look fine."

They sat for a while enjoying the coolness while Anna slowly regained her strength.

Finally, Anna spoke, "Thank you, Lynch."

Lynch was embarrassed but he managed an answer. "I'm glad I could be of help." He was thankful she hadn't gone to see Susan by herself.

Anna struggled up to her feet saying she thought she was able to travel.

He asked if she was sure. She nodded. Lynch got the horses and helped her to mount, steadying her as he handed up the reins.

The rest of the trip was made in silence. Lynch started to speak once but decided against it.

When they reached the yard, Lynch got Scrugs, the cook, to stay with Anna. He then dispatched two riders; one to fetch Sam, the other one he sent to town.

He searched for two more riders, told them to get ice from the ice house where food was stored, put it in a wagon and go pick up Susan's body and take it to town.

He walked over to the main house to see Scrugs and find out how Anna was doing.

Scrugs assured him everything was fine. He had fixed her some tea and she was lying down resting.

Deciding he could do no more for the present, Lynch went into the bunkhouse, rolled a smoke, then poured himself a drink which he drank in one gulp. He could feel it burn all the way down.

3

Money Talks

SAM rode into the yard before dusk and sent for Lynch. They met on the porch. Sam motioned for Lynch to follow him into the house.

Sam walked over to the fireplace and snarled, "Where is Jake and my grandchildren?"

Lynch resented Sam's tone, said simply, "I sent Shorty into town to see what he could find out. That's all I can tell you, and Shorty hasn't got back yet."

Sam sat down, sensed the annoyance in Lynch, and in a calmer voice asked, "How did it happen; I mean, with Susan?"

"All I know is hearsay. Old Dobs said your daughter was climbing down from their wagon last week when the horses moved and pitched her out. She landed astraddle a wagon wheel. Been awful sick since then."

Sam sat slumped for a moment before saying, "Why didn't she send for me?"

Lynch stood silent for a moment gazing at the older man. He was loyal to Sam, but he did not like him. He said, "Maybe she was afraid."

Sam's eyes came up swiftly. "Afraid of what? Her own father for Chris'sake!"

Lynch stood his ground. "She knew how you felt about Jake. Maybe she thought there might be trouble if you two got together."

Sam's face reddened, his mouth pulled flat. "That worthless bastard! Trouble! There'll be trouble, Lynch! I want my grandchildren back!"

"They might already be out of the country, Mister Croft."

The older man's eyes were the colour of old iron. "That won't stop me. I'll find them." He would have said more except he was diverted by a shadow passing the window.

Sam arose, "If that's Shorty, bring him in here!"

Lynch obeyed returning with a rangerider who was clearly worried and slightly breathless. He glanced from Lynch to Sam clearing his throat before speaking. "No one in town knew anything, boss. I asked around the stores and all . . . They was awful sorry to hear about Miss Susan." Shorty eased his weight from one leg to the other before continuing. "I couldn't find out where he went with the kids, and I sure tried."

Shorty stood there, watching his employer, still slightly breathless.

Sam turned back to his chair but did not sit down. He shoved fisted large hands into trouser pockets and remained lost in thought for a while. When he faced his rangemen again his eyes squinted as he said, "Shorty, go find those two Texas gunhands, Roberts and Coombs . . . And bring back Dutchy and Peters with you. That ought to be enough."

Shorty headed for the doorway obviously relieved to be leaving the room. After his departure Lynch looked steadily at Sam Croft as he quietly asked, "What do you have in mind?"

"Bring 'em back. What else would you expect me to do?"

Lynch dryly replied, "Yeah. Well, you want me to go along with 'em?"

"No. We'll be short-handed with four gone trackin'. It's time for the gather, which will take a couple of weeks. Lynch, you're the only one I can depend on to mind things here at the yard . . . you're foreman from now on. I can't do all this by myself."

Sam turned to his desk, poured two shot-glasses full of rye whiskey, turned back and offered one to Lynch.

"To my new foreman."

Lynch accepted the glass, unaware that Anna Croft was standing in the doorway behind him. He was thoughtfully holding the glass when his employer sharply said, "Anna, what do you want? I thought you were lying down."

Anna stood motionless watching her husband from tear-swollen eyes. "I no longer felt like lying down, Sam."

Sam paused to down his jolt of whiskey then said, "I'm expecting some rough men, Anna. You'd better run along."

She did not move. "Pretend I'm not here."

Sam's gaze hardened toward her. "It's better if you went back to your room and rested some more."

Her reply made Lynch turn and gaze at her.

"I prefer to stay."

Lynch had never seen her face her husband like this. Evidently it hadn't happened often because Sam looked surprised.

He sputtered, "Anna . . . "

"I'm going to stay, Sam."

Sam's fist closed around the whiskey glass until the knuckles were white.

"Go back to your room, Anna!"

"And if I don't Sam? Will you hit me the way you did Jake when he asked you if he could marry Susan?"

Lynch could see the explosion coming and leaned to set aside the untouched glass he had been holding, but Anna yielded before Sam could answer.

"I'll go . . . Sam . . . don't do something you'll regret the rest of your life." She looked at Lynch, then turned and walked out of the room.

Lynch's discomfort was acute. He was embarrassed at having witnessed this clash between his employer and his employer's wife, but more than that, he was troubled by the look in Anna's eyes.

When Lynch faced Sam again, he had difficulty maintaining the aloofness it had been his policy to practise toward things on the ranch which did not concern him. In a very even voice he said, "She was the one who found Susan dead over there, Mister Croft."

Sam brushed that aside. "She'll get

25

over it. She's been blaming me ever since she got back from Susan's. Not in words, Lynch, but I know my wife, she'll get over it." He turned when sounds became apparent on the porch. "Shorty's back with the others. Let 'em in."

In Lynch's absence, Sam retrieved his whiskey glass, re-filled it and dropped the contents straight down. When the weathered, lean and hard-faced rangemen entered ahead of Lynch he made an expansive gesture for them to be seated. He was brisk, practical, steel-eyed Sam Croft again.

Without any preliminaries he addressed the two Texans, "I have a job for you. I want you to find my grandchildren and bring them back here to the ranch. There'll be good pay for each of you when you return with 'em."

One of the lanky Texans, the one named Coombs, spoke frankly, "Supposin' your son-in-law don't want to give them up, Mister Croft?"

Sam met the Texan's impersonal

gaze with one just as impersonal. "Do whatever you got to do. Just bring those children back. Is that clear?"

"Clear enough, Mister Croft."

Roberts, the other Texan had a question. "Just how much money are we talkin' 'bout, Mister Croft?"

Sam's eyes shot daggers when he gruffly answered. "Eight hundred dollars. Four hundred for each of you."

"That's two hundred for each child," a bittersoft voice spoke from the doorway.

All heads turned toward the doorway. Anna Croft was standing there with a half-grim smile, eyeing each man in the room.

Sam started to speak but under the circumstances thought better of it.

No one said a word as she entered the room and sank down into the nearest chair.

Sam began apologizing for his wife's behaviour after what she'd been through, when he was brought up short with Anna's next statement.

"Shut up Sam. Don't make a fool of yourself. I'm in perfect control of myself which is more than I can say for you."

For lack of something to say, Sam said, "I thought you were resting in your room."

"Well, as you can see, I'm not."

The silence was deafening. Rangeriders were not used to this sort of thing. They did not move a muscle.

Finally, Anna spoke directly to Sam. "You won't give up this hunt for the children?"

"No."

"It's possible for them to begin a new life somewhere else." Anna said.

"They belong here!"

"Because you say so?"

"No. Because they are my grand-children."

Anna countered, "They are also my grandchildren."

"I didn't mean to imply . . . "

"Answer me one question, Sam. When was the last time you went to

28

see your grandchildren?"

Sam had no reply.

"Well, I went two or three times a month."

Sam's jaw dropped. He was dumbfounded. How could he have not known she had deliberately disobeyed him?

Anna went on. "They were a complete joy. It's too bad you didn't get to know them, spend some time with them . . . If I can let them go Sam, why can't you?"

He found his voice. "No. Never."

"Is that your final word?"

"It is."

Anna changed the mood by looking at the other men in the room.

"Gentlemen," she said in a firm voice. "I'm also offering eight hundred dollars . . . "

"Ma'm," Coombs said. "We already accepted your husband's offer."

"Let me finish, Mister Coombs. I'm offering eight hundred dollars to see that no harm comes to my son-in-law Jake, or his children."

"How would you know we didn't harm him, Missus Croft?"

"Because you'll bring him back with the children, Mister Coombs."

Quietness pervaded while the bizarre situation was pondered by the Texans.

Sam said, "You're crazy Anna. Why are you doing this?"

"To make sure no harm comes to the children's father." She considered the Texans. "Well, gentlemen, do we have a bargain?"

The men looked at each other, finally nodding, neither speaking or looking at Sam, who was boiling inside but said nothing.

Anna arose, excused herself and left the room. For a long moment after her departure there was silence, then Coombs said, "Mister Croft, does your wife have that kind of money? I never knew a woman who did."

Sam scoffed. "Of course not."

Coombs arose. "We'll bring 'em back for you. Time to turn in, good night."

4

A Helping Hand

JAKE was awakened by wind whistling through pine trees. He had dreamed of Susan, his arms aching to hold her; but when he got close to her, she told him it was time to be on their way, to hurry.

A waving pine bough kept flickering sunlight into his eyes so he got up, went to the little fresh water creek and splashed cold water into his face, then walked over to the top of the slope where he could view the valley below.

Gazing into the distance, the valley looked peaceful, but he knew it was just a matter of time before there was pursuit.

His eyes showed signs of fear, then anger mixed with hatred, and finally determination. He knew he had his hands full. Tough enough for one man to try to escape pursuers — let alone a man with four young ones and an old wagon.

Jake hitched the horses before he awakened the children. He was proud of the way they had taken on responsibilities. Joseph had filled the water barrels and canteens. Sarah was watching their food supplies and taking care of Lottie. William had spent time pulling grass by the creek and stuffing it into a burlap bag 'just in case the horses get hungry' he had proudly announced.

The going was easier now. They had camped on the summit and from here on it was all downhill. The land rolled gently, and the lower they got the warmer it became.

They stopped only briefly now and then to rest the horses, and to stretch their legs.

They munched on jerky and dried apples while travelling. It was long after sundown before Jake finally stopped for the night.

With the children bedded down inside the wagon, Jake tossed his bedroll under the wagon. He managed short periods of sleep, but was instantly alert at the slightest sound. Once he raised his head, cocking it in the direction of what appeared to be the faint whinny of a horse.

They were on the trail before sunup. Sarah asked if she could sit beside her father for a while since Joseph was walking alongside and William and Lottie had been lulled back to sleep in the wagon bed. Jake answered by making room for her.

Sarah was quiet, often glancing sideways at her father. Aware of this, Jake asked, "Somethin' on your mind, honey?"

At first Sarah was thoughtful, seeking courage to put into words — feelings that wouldn't hurt her father. "I'm gonna miss seeing grandma."

Jake agreed. "I will too. She's a wonderful woman."

"But most of all I'm gonna miss

Mama." She hurriedly went on before Jake could speak. "But I know she is in a better place and she isn't in any pain. In fact she's probably lookin' down on us right now," she said leaning over and looking up.

"I'm sure she is, Sarah, and I know she's mighty proud of you right now . . . " Jake's voice trailed off. This was a painfully difficult conversation.

"I feel better now," Sarah said. "Mama always said talking helps a person to feel better."

Jake smiled, put an arm around Sarah and agreed. "It does help."

The sun was low on the horizon when they stopped to camp for the night. Jake built a fire and they had their first warm meal in two days.

The night chill pressed close with the fading twilight. Jake wrapped Sarah and Lottie in blankets and quilts, arranging the boys in like fashion, positioning them around the campfire. They were asleep in minutes.

In the ensuing silence, Jake's thoughts

turned to Susan, he was conscious of a desperate loneliness. He fought off the feeling and tried to sleep. Susan returned to his thoughts — like a warning. Instantly he was no longer tired or sleepy. He rolled out of his bedroll, slipped on his boots, fastened on his gun-belt and faded into the darkness.

He backtracked to the top of the last knoll and scanned the trail they had travelled that day, and saw a flickering light, which meant a campfire. He judged it to be four to five miles away. His initial reaction was fear. There was not a shred of doubt about the men that campfire belonged to, or about the man who had sent them. His heart pounded as he headed back to camp.

Jake quietly hitched the horses, then carefully lifted the children into the back of the wagon. He threw some dirt on the campfire, climbed up onto the seat and started the horses on a slow walk.

His mind raced. He hadn't figured on them finding Susan for another day at least. His chance of getting out of the territory were down to zero. A simple fact forced him to change his plans; No loaded wagon on earth could out-run saddlehorses.

Jake mulled over alternatives. He could find a place for an ambush — but he didn't know how many men were following him. He was very good with a rifle, but not with a sixgun. There was also the threat to the children. He didn't want to expose them to danger and that left only one solution — he had to leave them somewhere.

He remembered a fair-sized town approximately two or three miles down the road. He would take the children there and maybe some generous family would take them in for a while.

He continued planning. If he was lucky enough to find a family to keep the children, he could continue on with the wagon which no doubt his pursuers would follow not knowing he was alone. Perhaps, if he was fortunate enough to find a good spot for an ambush he could discourage his pursuers. Creases appeared in his forehead as he wondered again how many men were following them.

Practically every light was out when the wagon rolled into the town named Coldwater. Jake was in a dilemma where could he find a place to hide the children in a town he was unfamiliar with? He drove down the main thoroughfare glancing left to right. Then he saw it; a steeple with a house alongside, which was no doubt a parsonage. He stopped out front, got down stiffly from the wagon, drew in a deep, hopeful breath and walked up to the door of the parsonage.

He knocked. There was no response. He knocked again harder. He saw the light from a lamp that had been lit — and waited. A tall, thin, sleepy-eyed middle-aged man appeared in the doorway looking annoyed.

When Jake didn't speak, the tall man asked, "Well?"

"Are you the Reverend?"

Yes. Reverend Thomas Caldwell."

"I have an awful big favour to ask of you, Reverend Caldwell."

The Reverend waited.

"Do you have any children, Reverend?"

You got me up this time of night to ask if I have any children?" Reverend Caldwell asked in disbelief.

"I know it sounds strange, Reverend, but it really is important."

Reverend Caldwell stood staring. Finally he asked Jake what his name was.

"Jake."

"Do you have a last name?"

"Just Jake will do for now."

"Well, Jake, what is the big favour?"

"First answer my question. Do you have any children?"

"We have one daughter. Two sons died before they were a year old."

"Would you and your wife consider takin' in four young'uns for a spell? I'd pay you for your trouble and their keep. They're well mannered and . . . "

Reverend Caldwell stopped him by motioning him inside. "Start at the beginning."

Jake related all that had transpired the last few days, also filling him in on the pursuers and what he planned to do to keep them following the wagon; leaving out the part about the ambush.

Thomas Caldwell studied him in silence for what seemed ages to Jake. Finally, he asked a question. "And what should I do with them if you don't come back?

Jake lifted his head gazing directly into Reverend Caldwell's eyes as he answered. "Then it will become your decision to make. I don't have a chance in hell, excuse me Reverend, with the children. It's too dangerous a situation for them. With that burden off my mind, I'll be able to think and move faster . . . It would sure ease my mind if I knew they were being well cared for."

Reverend Caldwell said, "Four of 'em you say."

"Yes. Two boys and two girls. Joseph's ten, Sarah's eight, William's five, and Lottie's almost four."

"Let me get my wife, Mister . . . er . . . Jake. She'll make up some pallets for them tonight and arrange for some beds tomorrow. Then I'll help you carry them in."

"That won't be necessary, Reverend. I'll need to talk to them before I leave them with strangers . . . Another thing Reverend, would it be possible for you to keep them hidden for a couple of days? Just until I've lured away the pursuers?"

"That won't be easy," Reverend Caldwell replied. "Kids is kids, but I'll try. I'll fetch my wife."

Jake strode back to the wagon with lightened shoulders, awakened the children and had a long talk with them.

Sarah threw her arms around Jake and held tightly to him. She was on the verge of crying.

Jake assured her that Reverend Caldwell and his wife would take good care of them while he was gone and that they had a daughter she could become friends with.

Sarah said, "We've lost Mama, we don't want to lose you too."

Jake kissed her cheek as he said, "I'm sure gonna do everything I can to see that don't happen," and with a twinkle in his eye, "Maybe you can get Reverend Caldwell to pray for me."

"Oh, I will. I will."

"Now, grab some of your clothes and Lottie's doll, and we'll go inside where they're waiting for you."

The Reverend's wife was half as tall as her husband. She stood next to him wearing a robe, her hair in long braids. She smiled at the children. They smiled back — sheepishly.

Her voice was friendly. "For starters, you can call me Aunt Fannie. That way people around town won't be asking questions, all right?"

They nodded, said goodbye to their father and followed her into one of the bedrooms.

Jake handed a small roll of greenbacks to Caldwell saying. "I really appreciate this Reverend."

"Just come back for 'em. I'll pray for you."

"One other thing, Reverend. I need a horse. Can you direct me to the livery barn?"

"It's down on the right side of the road. At the end of town. There's a lantern hangin' by the door. You can't miss it."

"Thanks."

"Good luck to you . . . and don't worry about the children. We'll take good care of them."

Jake headed in the direction of the livery barn with its dull lantern hanging to one side of the doorway. He found the night hostler leaning back against the wall in a rickety chair. His mouth open, expelling weird noises.

Jake tapped him on the shoulder

three times before the hostler opened his eyes, then jumped up almost knocking over the rickety chair.

"What can I help you with?" he mumbled, still not quite awake.

"I need to rent a horse for a couple of days," Jake replied. "Got one in good shape for ridin'?"

The hostler scratched his head, "Got a roan. Nice little gelding. Quick and sturdy as they come."

"Any others?" Jake queried.

"Nope. Only one that's for hire."

"Okay. Saddle and bridle come with it?"

"Yep."

You wouldn't happen to have a rifle scabbard around?" Jake asked.

"Have one that's sort of scratched up. A feller never came back for it," the hostler answered as he started away to get the roan horse.

After the horse was outfitted, the hostler held out his hand, "That'll be a dollar a day."

Jake counted out two dollars. "If it's

43

longer than two days, I'll pay the rest when I bring the horse back."

The night hostler nodded his head.

Jake led the horse to the wagon, tied it to the tailgate, climbed up on the wagon seat and slowly drove out of town. Once he looked back to the darkened house of Reverend Caldwell.

5

Pursuers

JACK ROBERTS and Dan Coombs hadn't tried manhunting for money before but both were excellent trackers. They had partnered-up several years before. They had good years and bad ones. Their speciality was horse-stealing. They had it down to a science. Once they had been caught in a surround of stockmen and would have been hanged on the spot if a straggling band of tomahawks hadn't come along, stopped to watch, and when the stockmen would have waited them out, nightfall arrived, Roberts and Coombs escaped.

They had covered a lot of territory at their trade, never stayed long in a place where they planned to do their speciality. In fact they had finished planning a raid on Croft's remuda when Sam's rider, Shorty found them and brought them back to the ranch with him.

After they left the Croft house they had a smoke in the quiet night and talked. Roberts liked Sam Croft's offer. He told Coombs they wouldn't make that much money if they rustled Croft's whole damned remuda.

Coombs nodded but he was thoughtful. After a time he looked at Roberts as he said, You don't figure that woman might have eight hunnert dollars? She seemed to be someone who didn't make talk just for the hell of it."

Roberts shrugged, killed his smoke ready to head for the bunkhouse. He wasn't interested in Anna, he was interested in some clod-hopping darned fool who thought he could get plumb away driving a loaded wagon, until his partner straightened up off the tie-rack as he said, "Jack; they got money. Look around. Four hired hands, land as far as a man can see. Good grade cattle."

Roberts said nothing. He knew from experience his partner had something in mind. Roberts waited.

"We'll find them kids and the clod-hopper. The old man wants his son-in-law taken care of. The woman don't. Now; suppose the son-in-law had some kind of accident."

"What'n hell would we do with four little kids?" Roberts asked, and got an annoyed look from Coombs as he explained. "We'd sell 'em."

Roberts stared.

"Sell 'em back to Mister Croft. He figures to pay two hunnert for each kid, which is a lot of money; suppose we told him the price for each kid would be a thousand dollars?"

Roberts continued to stare at his partner, but now a slow smile arrived and he nodded gently. You're thinking. All right. Now let's bed down so's we can get an early start."

They got an early start, so early none of the other sleepers heard them tip-toe outside before putting their boots on.

It was dark as the inside of a well, and cold. They were in the saddle before it was light enough to sashay until they found fresh wagon tracks. They found them miles west of the Croft yard, going north into the distant mountains. By daylight they were slouching along planning for what came next. Following steel tyre marks of a loaded wagon was as easy as falling off a log.

Coombs was contemptuous. "Clodhoppers! I never yet seen one that had the brains gawd give a chicken."

After nightfall they found a grassy clearing, built a small fire for warmth and ate jerky as tough as wood and drank creek water. It was a diet they had become accustomed to. Sometimes they growled about it but not this night. Four thousand dollars was more money than either of them had ever seen at one time in their lives.

Jack Roberts tossed wood into the fire making it spark and flare up as he said, "We ought to do this for a livin'."

Dan Coombs didn't answer. Sometimes his partner talked like a fool. How many times could a man fall into a situation like this, where feuding families would fight over children?

They rolled out at dawn, the trail was easy to follow, steel tracks had crushed pine needles every yard of the way. With a warming sun on their backs, and more jerky in their stomachs, they rode steadily at a walk. There was no need for haste, they were both well mounted and the track was fresh.

Roberts leaned often to scratch his leg. Coombs eventually asked what he was doing. "Something crawled into my bedroll last night an' bit me," Roberts answered.

Coombs had the answer. "I got some of that bear grease mixed with slick weed. Get down an' I'll smear some on it. It'll stop the itchin'."

Roberts dismounted. He was uncomfortable dropping his britches but he did it. Coombs brought forth a little dented tin from a saddlebag, liberally applied the grease, and said, "Must've been a baby scorpion."

"Don't feel like it was no baby one."

Coombs was stowing his dented tin when he answered. "It was a baby. If it'd been a full-grown one you wouldn't be ridin'."

Evidently the salve did what it was supposed to do. Roberts stopped favouring his leg.

They continued following the tracks without haste until they arrived at the place where Jack had made his first campfire. They scouted the area on foot until they had gleaned all the information they could find, then mounted and pushed ahead, still without haste. Coombs was of the opinion that the fugitives and their wagon were not far ahead.

Roberts made an off-hand remark. "Coldwater's up ahead. I'd guess from the way he's goin' he'll come down out of here, hit the Coldwater road, an' maybe head for stores down there."

Coombs did not disagree nor agree. In fact he said nothing, which encouraged his partner to expound further. "Someone up ahead's bound to have seen a wagon with kids in it."

Coombs finally broke his silence. "Jack, he's been movin' at night."

"Not always or he couldn't have got so far."

Coombs let the matter rest. As long as the tracks pointed in the direction of the town, he was content that one thing his partner had said was correct: A wagon with kids in it in a town would be noticed.

They did not reach Coldwater until mid-afternoon. They left their animals to be cuffed, grained and hayed when they split up, one on each side of the road, seeking information about a clod-hopper in a wagon with four children.

When they met back at the livery barn with no worthwhile information, the liveryman, who had been absent when they arrived, sent his swamper to do chores and greeted Roberts and Coombs genially out front of the runway.

They asked him about a sod-buster with four children and he hung fire over his answer so long it seemed he might not answer at all before he slowly shook his head and said, "Nope. If you boys are lookin' for him maybe he didn't come this way. It's a big country."

"He come this way, mister. We been trackin' him since early yestiddy mornin'," Coombs exclaimed.

The liveryman, a large, burly man of middle years with a full beard and dark eyes again hung fire before speaking. "Did you ask around town?"

Roberts nodded.

"An' no one remembers him?"

Again Jack Roberts nodded without speaking, and this time the liveryman seemed encouraged. "Take a little more time, gents. If he came through Coldwater, someone had to see 'em.

Try the smith across the road. Maybe the old woman who runs the hotel; that'd be a likely place for someone with children."

Coombs regarded the large, bewhiskered man in silence for a few moments, then jerked his head at Jack Roberts. "Let's get on our way."

Jack dug in his heels. "I'm goin' eat first."

They crossed to the cafe, which was half full, got two places at the counter and ordered. Strangers in any small town were a novelty. They were conscious of covert stares. When food came they ignored everything else. Jerky and branch water kept a man alive but that's about all it did.

When they finally left Coldwater on the southerly coach road their confidence faded a little. The roadbed had tyre marks; narrow buggy tracks, six-inch freighter tracks, saddle horse tracks by the dozen.

One set interested Dan Coombs. It was the right size and a mile or so below Coldwater it veered to the left. The tracks headed directly toward a boulder field of about twenty acres. Even a rider would avoid that place. Someone driving a wagon wouldn't try to navigate his way through those closely-jumbled acres of large rocks if he had a lick of sense, and Coombs had no reason to think Jake was that inexperienced. He might not know the country though.

They followed the tracks easterly from the road. The land gradually tipped, it did not get steep but where it topped-out was where the boulder field was.

It was open country all the way, no trees, no thickets, only drying grass and an occasional boulder which may have rolled down from the field of stones.

The evening was advancing, it would be cooler in another hour or so. Coombs rode with a puckered brow; unless there was a trail through that jumble of large boulders, whoever had driven that wagon, and he felt certain he knew who it was, could not possibly take a four-wheeled vehicle any farther than the rocks up ahead.

What kept Coombs pondering was the set of saddle-horse tracks directly between the rear wheel-marks of the wagon. He finally drew rein, sat with both hands atop the saddlehorn gazing up where the wagon tracks led. He said, "Jack, I'm beginnin' to wonder if we ain't been led on a goose chase."

"Why?"

"He had a saddle animal tied to his tailgate. My guess is that he went up into them rocks, took the saddle horse and left the wagon for us to find."

Roberts had a different notion. "Or he's hid in them rocks watchin' us."

Because Coombs did not believe this he said, "Let's find out," and resumed riding.

6

Complications

THEY rode cautiously. For one thing they did not know their man. For another, although homesteaders were known to be better with plough handles than with weapons, there were exceptions and this one might be an exception.

Coombs was breasting the boulder plateau when he abruptly reined to a halt. There was an old wagon with a home-made texas over ash bows sitting about a hundred yards ahead without horses on the pole. They sat a long time in silence before Roberts said, "He could be hidin' among them big rocks anywhere. He was a fool to come up here."

"My guess," stated Coombs, "is that he didn't know the country. You can't see how close them big rocks is to one another from back down yonder."

"Well; if he's watchin' us, an' if he's got a weapon, it wouldn't be real smart to go pokin' among them rocks, would it?"

Coombs did not answer. He was faintly scowling as he continued to search for signs of people or their movement. Roberts got restless. "We're settin' out here like pigeons, Dan."

Still Coombs said nothing. He gradually became about half convinced that since the wagon had been stuck amidst the boulders for a long time, the homesteader and his brood had fled on foot.

He nudged his horse forward in the direction of the wagon, Roberts raised an arm. Two thirteen-hundred pound harness horses were grazing hobbled about a quarter mile from the wagon.

Roberts darkly scowled. "Why didn't he take them with him? Hell, a man with four kids . . ."

"They ain't broke to ride, that's

why." Coombs said curtly, and he was right, there were very few combination horses especially if they were as large and broad as Jake's animals were.

They reached the wagon without incident. Roberts was shaking his head as he swung off. In his opinion this Jake-feller was some kind of a danged fool to let himself get bottled up like this.

Roberts went over to climb up and look inside. As he was climbing down he said, "It's them all right. Kids' clothes and a couple of bedraggled dolls, some furniture and other junk."

Jack Roberts was toeing into his stirrup to mount when the silence was broken by a loud, slamming gunshot. The horn cap was torn off Coombs' saddle. His mount gave a tremendous jump, as did Roberts' horse. Roberts, with one foot off the ground, went down on his back but he clung to his left rein. Coombs was too busy controlling his animal to do anything else. He was still occupied with the frightened horse when the second gunshot thundered loudly. Anyone with a lick of sense would know whoever was shooting had a rifle, not a six-gun nor a carbine, and that was consistent with homesteaders. But they were very rarely as good a marksman as this one was. He hadn't tried to kill anyone, but clearly he could have, both Coombs and Roberts were exposed.

Roberts arose, did not bother dusting himself off but squared around in a slight crouch, mad as a hornet. Coombs was still atop his horse, as fine a target as anyone could desire. He called sharply to his partner. "Don't shoot!"

Roberts snarled his reply. "Shoot what? Where is the son of a bitch?"

That was the reason Coombs had called; he could not be sure of the location of the shots, they had both been too busy with their startled animals.

Finally, Roberts brushed himself off and re-shaped his hat. He was still mad as a hornet. In their years of association Dan Coombs had learned to understand his partner. When Jack Roberts was angry he didn't use good sense.

Before Roberts could start an unequal gunfight and maybe get them killed, Coombs told him to get on his horse, which he did, still fierce-eyed and red-faced.

Coombs led the way back down away from the boulder field. When they were back on the road heading toward Coldwater, he said, "When it's dark enough we'll get him."

"How?"

"With four little kids he can't travel much at night. Specially if some of them is real young. We can hear four kids stumblin' around in the dark, and whatever-his-name-is can't shoot what he can't see."

"His name is Jake."

"All right, Jake. We'll sneak back down here later. Right now I'm hungry an' thirsty."

Roberts brightened slightly. He was thinking of the Coldwater saloon across from the stage company's corralyard.

Darkness arrived with a skimpy moon while they were at the cafe. Hungry men concentrate on eating. Otherwise Coombs and Roberts might have noticed there was almost no conversation while they were eating, and that several of the other diners were warily studying them.

They had completely missed the significance of the liveryman's hesitating conversation with them, but a whisper had passed through Coldwater that two mean-looking riders had asked around town about a sod-buster with a wagon and four children.

What bothered the burly liveryman was that after he had let the homesteader take his grey horse, and the manhunters had asked around town about a man with a wagon with four children in it, he had not seen any children in the wagon. In a city that would have amounted to an insignificant mystery, in a place like Coldwater, whose total population was no more than three, maybe four hundred people, where everyone knew everyone else's business, it was something to capture and hold attention.

The whisper had spread and had temporarily died until the two mean-looking, raffish strangers returned, then it flared up again.

Later, up at the saloon Coombs and Roberts took a bottle to a distant table and relaxed. Eventually Coombs thought the saloon was quiet compared to most he'd been in, and looked around.

The bar had about eight or ten loungers along it. There was a game of Pedro at a table near the stove. The barman was as solemn as an owl. Coombs felt uncomfortable but Roberts noticed nothing, he was enjoying his whiskey on a full stomach.

Later, tired enough to take their bedrolls out behind the livery barn and roll in, the conversation up at the saloon picked up. Some rangemen among the customers were indifferent but most of the townsmen were very curious. They were only marginally concerned with two hardcased tracking a farmer, but a farmer clearly fleeing from some kind of pursuit with four youngsters was different. They did not like the odds nor the danger to the youngsters, most of them had families of their own.

Small towns had a tendency to take sides on emotional rather than logical grounds. Coldwater was no exception.

With justification, seeing that they had been in the saddle so long and had stuffed themselves at the cafe, Coombs and Roberts over-slept.

Roberts awakened with a thin sliver of feeble grey beginning to streak the eastern horizon. He swore, jerked his partner awake and stood to stamp into his boots.

Dan Coombs reacted the same way. It would be full daylight before they got down to the boulder field. The clod-hopper would be long gone, even with four youngsters — unless he also over-slept, which Coombs would not have bet on.

Roberts was disgruntled. He said, "Hell, we might as well have breakfast. It won't make no difference, it'll be sunup anyway."

Coombs thought about this, shrugged and followed his partner. The cafeman had just fired up his stove and lighted a lamp. They were his first customers. He greeted them with a nod, took their orders and scuttled to his cooking area. A tall, sinewy man with grey at the temples came in, gazed at the strangers, nodded and went to the far curve of the counter. He had 'cowman' written all over him.

Roberts leaned to half whisper. "We'll get him. With kids an' bein' on foot in rough country We'll get him."

Coombs glared at his partner. The cafe was as quiet as a tomb.

They left Coldwater with an ascending

sun rising ponderously off in the east. The road was shadowed and would remain that way for a while.

Behind them there was a small flurry of excitement. The tall, greying man who had entered the cafe was Coldwater's constable. He rarely wore his badge; he had been the local lawman since Hector had been a pup, everyone knew him, except for strangers he didn't have to wear his badge. His name was Denton Wright.

What caused the shock after Coombs and Roberts had resumed their manhunt had nothing to do with them. Not directly anyway. It had to do with the preacher, who had one youngster. She was noisily playing in the yard with several children no one had seen before. There were four of them. It did not require great deductive powers to form up a strong enough suspicion for the constable to go up to the preacher's place and confirm the identity of four strange youngsters.

The best attitude in a cow-town was the degree of ambivalence townsfolk had toward squatters. People either liked them individually or tolerated them, but on Saturdays when rangemen came to town the subject of homesteaders was avoided; they did not contribute much to the Coldwater economy, but every little bit helped.

It was early in the week when Constable Wright explained at the saloon what he had figured out was happening, and no one bothered to ask why manhunters were searching for the sod-buster, they were troubled that four small children were involved.

By the time the sun was high and Coombs with his partner was carefully exploring the boulder field for tracks, folks in Coldwater had their minds pretty well made up. Whatever crime the sod-buster had committed, his children were not going to be part of it.

It was a hot day. The heat this time of the year would last well into the night. Large rocks absorbed heat and reflected it. It did not help that the air was not stirring nor that neither of the manhunters came across a sign of water.

They found tracks, but of one man, and he had evidently been coyote because there was only an occasional boot-print. He had jumped from rock to rock. They lost his sign for a while before Roberts found one of those places where he'd had to cross dusty earth because the rocks were too far apart.

He seemed to be making a deliberate wide half circle, Coombs stopped, mopped off sweat and said, "I think he's makin' a big sashay that'll take him back to Coldwater."

Roberts was scowling. "Where are the kids? They can't jump from rock to rock like he done." Roberts straightened in the saddle squinting hard in all directions. "He hid 'em."

Coombs snorted derisively. "Where? In these rocks with no grub or water?

Even if he did, they'd make noise, cry or somethin'."

"Well, where are they?"

"Hid for a fact, but I don't think he hid 'em out here."

"Where, dammit!"

"I don't know, Jack."

"Back in town?"

Coombs sat in thought, made one swipe at the sweat on his forehead and faced his partner. "Maybe you're right. They sure as hell ain't out here."

They rode back to the wagon, rummaged it, found nothing they hadn't seen the day before, and picked their way slowly back out of the boulder field.

Roberts had a thought. "Maybe he knew someone down there who'd take the kids for him."

Coombs shrugged. He was a logical individual. Anyone who didn't know the country well enough to avoid getting blocked solid in a field of rocks, probably didn't know anyone in the Coldwater country. But he'd figured out why they'd gotten negative answers to their questions about someone passing through with a wagon: Jake had done it late at night.

They were half way back to Coldwater, both thirsty enough to spit cotton, before Coombs told Roberts his idea, Roberts nodded as he usually did when his partner seemed to have solved a problem, but he also wondered about something.

"Them folks is goin' to guess who we are an what we're doin' — tryin' to run down that danged squatter."

"Let 'em," Coombs shot back. "I never been in one of these cow-towns where folks didn't make up all sorts of stories whenever strangers ride in. What we got to do, Jack, is find them kids. To hell with the squatter; them kids is worth four thousand dollars to us."

When they reached Coldwater, sweaty, hot, hungry and thirsty, they headed for the saloon first, quenched their thirst with beer then went down to the cafe. Both places were nearly empty, it was too close to suppertime for the locals to be much in evidence.

The first surprise they got was later, after sundown, when they couldn't find their bedrolls until the burly liveryman came out back and roughly said. "If you're lookin' for your bedding. I rolled 'em and got 'em in the harness room."

Coombs recovered first from the chilly treatment. "It ain't a friendly town, Jack. Let's go up to the roomin' house. I'm tired of sleepin' on the ground anyway."

The treatment at the hotel was similar except that the proprietor was small, bird-like and timid. He told them all his rooms were taken, for which he expressed regret.

From the hotel proprietor's meekness Coombs thought he was probably telling the truth. It wasn't until they returned to the saloon after dark when the place had at least two dozen customers, that it dawned on Coombs the attitude of the town was definitely different than it had been when they had ridden south earlier in the day. He told Roberts he thought tomorrow they should camp north of town, up where there were some trees for shade and tall feed for their animals.

Jack was not so dense that he too hadn't sensed the change. They awakened before dawn and rigged out at the livery barn, lashed bedrolls behind cantles and rode side-by-side up the main thoroughfare of Coldwater at a dead walk going north. People were satisfied they were leaving the country. As some recalled, they had come from the north. Now, evidently, they were going back the same way.

The morning was cool with a bright sun shining. That would change when the sun was overhead, but they rode several miles before the heat came, set up camp a half mile or so from the stageroad near water, good graze, and abundant shade in a bosque of white oaks. To men of their kind, the camp was preferable to the town. Towns were places where a man could sleep up off

71

the ground, get fed well, and replenish supplies, otherwise they cramped men accustomed to open country.

Coombs had been thinking on the leisurely ride. He eventually said, "Jack, them kids is in Coldwater somewhere as sure as you're a foot tall. The sod-buster's still out there somewhere, which it seems to me he'd be because he don't want to get too far from his children, and also because them two big pudding-footed draft horses of his is still hobbled in the rock field. That horse he trailed off the tailgate had small feet, it wasn't no draft animal. His tracks was too small, it was a saddle horse. An' somethin' else he knows we're lookin' for him."

Roberts looked sceptical. "Why'd he get the saddle animal unless he aimed to abandon the wagon and try to out-run us on horseback?"

Coombs sank into another long period of thoughtful silence, then brightened. "He knows we're after him. Y'see? Sure as hell he thinks we're after him personal." Coombs broadly smiled. "The hell with him. If he high-tails it out of the country all the better. We got to find his kids and I'll bet you a new hat they're down there in Coldwater."

"How do we find 'em?"

Again Coombs was silent for a spell. "I don't know, but four new kids in a place like Coldwater . . . " Coombs stopped in mid-sentence. "Hell; where would you go to leave four youngsters in a place no bigger'n Coldwater?"

Roberts answered predictably. "I don't know. Maybe some family he knows."

"Or if he don't know anyone over here, there ain't many families who'd take in four young'uns. One maybe but not four. A good Christian family would . . . You seen that white-painted church at the north end of town?"

"Yes."

"Maybe I'm wrong but I figure only a real good gawd-fearin' family would take four youngsters in. Sure as hell that sour-faced liveryman wouldn't nor the saloonman, nor . . . Jack, we got to start our search with the preacher."

Roberts rode in silence for a hundred yards then shrugged. "We don't know what they look like."

For some reason that remark irritated Coombs. "Dammit, I told you four little strangers in Coldwater would be wondered about."

They set up their camp, nodded away the hottest part of the day in shade, had a typically meagre rangeman's supper and tried to figure out how to find four youngsters who had very recently come to Coldwater.

The problem was a difficult one. Without their knowledge it was going to resolve itself.

7

The Townspeople of Coldwater

REVEREND CALDWELL was sitting on a stool in front of a tall desk-like table, pen poised, writing a sermon for the Sunday service when he heard a rapping at the door. He sighed and put the pen down as he arose and went to the front door.

There was no one there.

There were times when he was called upon for the sick, dying or needy. Sometimes people brought baskets of vegetables from their gardens. Sometimes even a chicken was left on the doorstep. But now he saw none of these things.

He looked right and left, saw no one, closed the door and went back to his stool.

He had just got settled when the

rapping came again. He was becoming a little irritated when the rapping became louder. It was coming from the back door, not the front door.

"Hold on," he called. "I'm coming."

At first his face showed shock, then he quickly opened the door wide and hurried the man inside the house, looked around outside, then spoke as he turned to face the man, "I didn't expect you back so soon."

Jake replied, "I didn't expect to be. How're the kids?"

"Fine. Just fine. Fannie took them out on a picnic back in the trees where there's a meadow and a little creek. A preacher has to have a little quiet to prepare a sermon."

Jake nodded again.

As the preacher went for the mugs he said, "Couple of cookies to go with the coffee?"

"That would be nice."

Reverend Caldwell put some cookies on a plate, set it on the kitchen table along with two mugs of coffee, pulled out a chair and nodded for Jake to do the same.

After Jake had eaten four cookies and taken a couple of sips of coffee, Thomas Caldwell said, "Care to talk about it?"

"Well," Jake started out slowly, "they followed the wagon all right. When they come up to it I was in the boulder field above them. I could have killed both of 'em."

The preacher put a hard gaze on Jake as he said, "But you didn't."

Jake was slow in replying. "It was a temptation, Reverend . . . but I'm not a murderer, and I knew it wouldn't end there. If I was caught I'd lose my children."

"So. What did you do?"

"I shot close to one of them figuring they wouldn't try again until after dark. Then I high-tailed it back here. They won't begin lookin' for me until tonight. Then they'll come back to town."

Thomas Caldwell studied Jake while

rubbing his chin. He always rubbed his chin when he was in deep thought. After a while he slapped Jake on the shoulder and said, "Well for starters, you'll stay here along with your children. The people in this town respect this house as a kind of sanctuary. I'll do some talkin' with the folks around town . . . the rest we'll leave in God's hands."

"Do you have any work needin' done?" Jake asked. "I'm good at fixin' fences, patchin' roofs, whatever."

"For a fact," the preacher replied, "I need some firewood split for the stove. Fannie's always after me for that. You'll find everythin' you need in the woodshed."

"I'm much obliged for everything," Jake said.

"I'm much obliged to you . . . you just provided me with my Sunday mornin' sermon."

Jake puzzled over that as he went out back to start splitting wood.

By the time the Reverend's wife returned with the children there was enough wood split for the wood box inside, a pile in the shed and enough kindling for a month.

The children scrambled over their father while he tried to explain to the Reverend's wife the present situation of having another house guest, feeling embarrassed as he was telling her.

Fannie eyed the wood box, knowing it was not the work of her husband, smiled her agreement of the situation and said, "We're pleased to have you . . . Jake? What is your last name?"

Jake laughed. "You won't believe this ma'm, but it's the same as yours, Caldwell."

"Sake's alive." As an afterthought she said, "Maybe we're kin?"

"I doubt it," Jake answered truthfully, "I don't recall my folks ever mentioning havin' a Reverend in the family."

She chased the children outside except for Sarah and her own daughter, whose name was Faye, with the excuse of preparing the evening meal.

Reverend Caldwell had been busy.

He stopped in at a few of the businesses setting up a meeting at his place after the supper hour and asked that the word be passed along to those he had missed. Everyone he talked to had an inkling of what he had in mind.

When the Caldwells had finished dinner, Fannie put the younger ones to bed which proved to be an easy chore after being outside all day on a picnic. The older children helped clear the table and were busy scrubbing pots and pans when she returned from bedding down the younger ones. She smiled, told them they had done a good job, gave them each a cookie and sent them off to bed.

Fannie's cheeks were rosy. She was happy having a houseful of children. The only child they'd had that had lived was Faye. Faye was nine years old.

People started arriving shortly after sundown. Fannie took them to the parlour and introduced them to Jake.

It wasn't long before the room was filled. Jake was touched. He was a total stranger to these people but they treated him as if they had known him all their lives.

Reverend Caldwell stood up and raised his hands for silence. He related Jake's story from beginning to end leaving nothing out. When he was finished, it was very quiet.

The liveryman broke the silence, "I'll fetch your wagon and team back to town in the morning."

That started the women talking among themselves. They would bring baskets of food to help the Caldwells feed five extra people.

George Mello, the general store owner spoke with a serious edge in his voice. "There was a man an' a woman come in this mornin' askin' whether a man with four young'uns had been in for supplies. I didn't know at the time."

"Are they still in town?" Jake wanted to know.

"Don't know for sure. They asked about the hotel."

"Can you describe them?" Jake asked.

The description matched Anna Croft and the hired hand Lynch Miller. Jake was totally surprised.

Al Johnson, the liveryman, piped up that they still had their horses stalled at the livery barn, therefore they must still be in town.

Jake took over the conversation. "I'm more'n obliged to all of you to take in strangers like this 'specially when none of this is your affair. The two men after us got to be hired-hands for Sam Croft. My first concern is for my children; secondly is that none of you get hurt."

One old man, stringy but sound-looking broke in, "Mister, we've all seen our share of troubles. We don't run from 'em. All right with you Reverend if we make this sort of our headquarters?"

"All right with me, Jacob. People are

comin' and goin' here all the time," Thomas Caldwell answered, thinking of the sermon he had just written.

The meeting began to break up; men shook hands with Jake, some murmured words of encouragement, nodding to Reverend Caldwell as they went out the door. Those with wives who were talking to Fannie Caldwell finally took their wives arms and also departed.

When all was quiet again Thomas Caldwell asked his wife if she would bring them a glass of her homemade blackberry wine.

She nodded and went to the kitchen.

Jake raised his eyebrows as he looked at the preacher.

As if reading Jake's mind Thomas Caldwell assured him they did not approve of drinking, but a glass of wine now and then was good for a person; besides it was Fannie Caldwell's own homemade wine and she was very proud of it.

She returned with three glasses

half full of a burgundy coloured wine, passed them around, kept one for herself as she sat down on a rocking chair.

Jake sipped the wine which was a little too sweet for him, but smiled and praised it nevertheless.

Reverend Caldwell spoke thoughfully, "I think the meetin' went pretty good. It helps if folks know what's going on."

Jake was scowling, "One thing puzzled me Reverend. What's my wife's mother and the rangerider Lynch Miller doin' here? Sam Croft would never let her come this far without him. Even with the rangerider along, he wouldn't allow it."

The preacher was not worried. "With all our ears open, we'll find out sooner or later. Right now we'd better turn in. It's been a long day."

Fannie Caldwell arose from the rocking chair; the day plus the wine had taken its toll. She said good night and headed for the bedroom.

The men said good night also; Reverend Caldwell following Fannie into their bedroom, Jake bedding down with Joseph and William.

Jake thought he wouldn't be able to sleep when he thought of the meeting and the faces of the people who had attended; but being tired, and perhaps because the glass of wine helped, he was oblivious to everything until the following morning.

Fannie had breakfast on the table when Jake appeared after washing up out back. "Go ahead and eat, Jake. Everyone else has been fed. We let you sleep. Just this once though," she told him as she filled his coffee mug.

He hurried and ate, took his plate and eating utensils over to the stove where a large wash basin was filled with other dirty dishes.

"Thomas is in his study re-writing his sermon with orders not to be disturbed; the boys are playing in back and I sent Faye, Sarah and Lottie over to Missus Johnson's for a basket of food she promised to send over when she left last night."

Jake told Fannie he thought he would go down to the livery barn and ride out with Al Johnson to bring back the wagon and team.

Fannie nodded as she bustled around the kitchen.

Jake saddled his rented horse and led it southward in the direction of the livery barn taking the precaution of using the back alley.

Al Johnson was just saddling a brown horse who had seen better days, but was in good shape, when Jake entered through the back runway.

They nodded to one another. Jake said, "I hate to trouble you to go all the way out there to bring in my wagon and team. I can go get it an' tie this horse on the tailgate like before."

Al Johnson studied Jake a moment before he replied. "That's a kindly offer, but with the constable out of town for a while, we sort of look to the Reverend for guidance. I don't think he'd take it kindly if I was to let you go alone. We'll go together and you can drive the wagon back. 'Sides I don't get out of town too often."

Jake didn't object. They mounted and rode out the back door of the livery barn.

The morning was beautiful. Not cold nor hot, though it would warm up considerably by the time they reached the wagon. They talked little but when they did it was friendly talk.

They reached the wagon as the sun was straight up in the sky.

Jake went to get the team of horses, found them where he had left them, by the grassy spot and a muddy little spring. He removed their hobbles, led them back to the wagon where Al Johnson helped with the hitching.

They tied both of their mounts to the tailgate, climbed up onto the wagon seat and started back to Coldwater.

The going was much slower than a-horseback but the men didn't mind.

By the time the rooftops of Coldwater

were in sight dusk was beginning to descend.

Al Johnson said, "Damned if I'm not hungry. Must be the fresh air."

Jake looked at Johnson's stocky build and thought he probably hadn't missed many meals. He smiled and said, "I could go for some food myself."

They agreed that the wagon and horses should be kept at the livery barn for the time being which meant taking a roundabout approach to come in the back way.

After unhitching the team and unsaddling the two mounts, Jake helped with the feeding before heading down the alley to the parsonage.

He walked into the kitchen after knocking and was faced with a chill of foreboding.

Reverend Caldwell was not there. His wife's eyes were swollen from crying. The tears flowed again as she kept saying over and over, "It's my fault. I never should have let them go."

Jake tried to make some sense out

of her babblings but got nowhere. He finally shook her, "Where is your husband?" he asked.

"At a town council meeting," she answered numbly.

"What's wrong?" Jake lightly shook her again.

She pointed to a piece of paper on the table. Jake picked it up, held it up to the light and read it aloud.

"We . . . have . . . your . . . two . . . girls. If you want to see them again . . . bring . . . four thousand dollars . . . to the tall pine tree five miles north of town . . . alone . . . in two days."

Jake's knuckles turned white as he crumpled the paper in his fist.

8

Disaster

AS Jake arose Fannie looked up with tearful eyes. "You don't think they will harm the girls, do you?"

He was still numb, mostly from surprise. It had not occurred to him that the men hunting for him would steal his children. He gazed blankly at the preacher's wife and shook his head. He asked her where the meeting was being held.

"At the general store." He was reaching for the door when she also said, "It's my fault, Jake. I'm terribly sorry."

After he had left Fannie gazed at the door briefly, then arose and became very busy. She couldn't get the disaster off her mind but she was old enough to know that being busy was the best alternative to self pity.

When Jake arrived at the general store there was a crowd, the building was noisy; both men and women were talking. Reverend Caldwell was trying to stop the racket. It wasn't an easy thing to accomplish until Jake walked in. Even those who didn't know him let the conversation die. Caldwell had told them Jake's story. He was the only stranger among them and the preacher greeted him somberly by name.

Jake glanced among the people and got a shock. Lynch Miller from the Croft ranch was among them. He approached Lynch to ask if he had come alone. He hadn't, Anna Croft had come with him. Jake did not look friendly which probably was what prompted Lynch to say, "She's at the hotel. It was a long ride. Those wagon tracks meandered all over hell."

"Those were the only tracks?" Jake asked.

Lynch slowly shook his head. "No.

Two riders followed the tracks all the way over here."

"Did you know if Sam sent them?"

"He did. I was at the ranch when Shorty brought them out, an' I saw them leave."

"Do you know them, Lynch?"

"I don't exactly know them but I know their names, one is called Dan Coombs, the other one is Jack Roberts." Lynch made a faint grimace. "From what I've heard they're penny-ante badmen. I've heard rumours about them. Sam put them on your tracks." Lynch gazed steadily at Jake over a silent moment, then spoke again. "We got here late last night. Anna was plumb tuckered. It's a long ride, Jake. We had no idea where your tracks were going to take us until this morning when we heard the talk. A little later I heard the worst of it. Coombs and Roberts have your little girls . . . Jake maybe I'm wrong, most likely I am, but right now it looks to me like maybe they wasn't ever after you, they was after the children."

"Why?" Jake asked and Lynch eyed him pensively as he replied. "For ransom, Jake."

Reverend Caldwell had the crowd quieted. He began his story with Jake's arrival in the night and ended it with the abduction of the children. Afterwards, even those who had surmised what was happening, or who had heard snatches of the situation which had arrived in their community out of the blue, were silent.

Jake turned to ask Lynch where Sam Croft was, and got an enigmatic answer. "Ask Miz Croft. She's restin' at the hotel. Jake, she don't know the girls are missing."

Jake didn't linger. He went up to the hotel near the north end of town, asked the timid proprietor which room Mrs Croft had, and climbed the stairs two at a time. He knocked on the door. When it opened Anna Croft was startled, but only for a moment before she pulled Jake into the room and closed the door.

Jake was brusque. "How come you to come over here?" he asked and before she could answer, he also asked her if her husband had come along.

Anna Croft went to one of two chairs in the room, sat and said, "Sam was out on the gather. I couldn't stand doing nothing. I brought Lynch along with me. Sam will have a fit when he returns."

Jake nodded about that; he would also fire Lynch for accompanying her.

She asked how the children were and if she could see them. Jake withheld nothing from her when he explained what had happened. He did not explain how it had happened because he did not know, but after thinking over what Lynch had said at the store, he made a guess when he said, "They're most likely goin' to hold the girls for ransom."

Anna Croft's colour faded, she was speechless for a long moment, then all she said was "Oh God."

Jake brought forth the crumpled note, smoothed it and handed it to her. She was still colourless as she read it, and afterwards repeated what she had said earlier, but this time looking unblinkingly at Jake.

"Oh God!" After a breathless moment she said, "They're just children. They'll hurt them, Jake."

"They'll die if they do," Jake replied. "But folks think they won't. They want a fortune for the girls. My kids are valuable to them."

"But, Jake, men like that . . . "

"Missus Croft, that's all I got to hang onto."

She said no more, but she sat slumped and old looking in the chair.

Jake sat down looking out the window, the shock had passed. To his knowledge there wasn't that much money in the world. He had reason to fear for his daughters. Lottie in particular was too young for any kind of abuse or hardship.

He came out of his reverie looking at

his mother-in-law. Anna looked about half ill. He asked if she'd like to see Joseph and William. She nodded dumbly, her eyes dark with pain and dread.

Jake arose. "The preacher's got them, an' right now his wife needs a friend. She blames herself for what happened."

"How did it happen, Jake?"

"All I know is that she sent them to a neighbour for something. Two men came along and took them. That's all I knew until I read the note."

Anna softly said, "Four thousand dollars? Even a bank wouldn't have that much money, Jake."

He nodded. "I know. It's crazy, but you read the note."

She arose. "I'd like to see the boys. Are they all right?"

Yes'm. It's not far, at the upper end of town by the church."

When they arrived at the Caldwell place Fannie was dry-eyed but just barely and as soon as Jake introduced the grandmother of his children the two women fell into each other's arms and cried.

Constable Denton Wright and a number of others had been conferring. There wasn't four thousand dollars in the entire town of Coldwater. A skilled artisan such as the blacksmith did not make that much in a year. Denton Wright told Jake folks could likely raise that much money but not in two days. Maybe not even in two weeks.

There had been talk of making up a posse and hunting down the abductors. The constable liked the idea, but was fearful for the little girls. He wondered if there wasn't some way to trick Coombs and Roberts. Jake shook his head. It was bad enough having his girls in their hands, but it might be a lot worse if the men who had them were made suspicious of some variety of a double-cross.

Jake would meet the abductors at the big pine tree. Lynch and the constable would leave in the night, be in position to shoot come morning.

Jake was worried. Going out there to beg for more time might be futile, in which case there would be a showdown.

He didn't tell anyone, particularly Anna Croft. He wasn't worried about the constable and Lynch so much as he was fearful about Coombs and Roberts. He did not know either men. He may have heard of them at some time but could not recall that happening.

One thing was abundantly clear: They were the kind of men who might, already begun to feel the money in their hands, just might not be above harming the children.

He did not sleep that night until along toward dawn when he dozed off for a couple of hours, until sunlight awakened him. He avoided the cafe; he did not want to listen to a lot of outrage and wild denunciation. He ate with the Caldwells. Anna was there along with Lynch and Jake's two boys. It was an awkward mostly silent meal.

Reverend Caldwell took Jake out back. "The men want to make up a posse," he said, and Jake's reaction startled the preacher.

"No! Don't let them do that! I'll ride out there alone this morning."

"Jake; they'll expect you to have four thousand dollars."

"I'll tell them I need more time. There isn't that much money in the countryside. They got to realise that, Reverend, they're hard men . . . Outlaws most likely. They got to know they can't just ride into new country and expect that much money to be handy. Reverend, don't let anyone ride out there. I got to do this alone. For the sake of my girls — I don't want a posse to go out there."

Reverend Caldwell nodded without speaking for a time, then he said, "Jake, we could probably find a thousand dollars, maybe even fifteen hundred. See if that'll let you have more time."

Jake nodded and the conversation terminated. He had not mentioned the scheme he, Lynch and the constable had worked out and right now, he wavered between trying the preacher's idea and going ahead with the other plan.

Fifteen hundred dollars was a small fortune, and it could just possibly buy more time. In the end he decided to try the other idea, relying on Lynch and the constable to be hidden and waiting when Coombs and Roberts arrived at the huge old pine tree five miles north of town.

He worried over his decision all day, and finally with the approach of evening he sought Lynch and the constable, told them what the preacher had said, and they both agreed it was a better idea, at least he could get fifteen hundred dollars, but they insisted on riding out tonight and being in bushwhacking position when the abductors arrived.

Jake yielded, worried that one way or another something would go wrong. If there was a gun fight, if both abductors were killed, how would he find his children? It was a vast and rugged country north of Coldwater.

Roiled nerves tired a man as much as missing too much rest. That night Jake slept like a baby. When he awakened he went down to the livery barn. The proprietor nodded his head at Jake's first question. "Yes. The constable an' that stranger you talked to yestiddy at the store, both left town last night in the dark." The liveryman was not at all dense, but he remained expressionless as he also said, "Mister, whatever happens, we're goin' to hang them sons of bitches." He was wrong.

Jake got the same roan horse from the liveryman and left town with sunlight of a cool morning making for a pleasant ride except that he did not realise it. His heart was in his throat. Maybe the abductors of his children would not be out there, the note had said two days, which could mean they wouldn't show up until tomorrow.

He was wearing his six-gun, although

he was not very fast nor accurate with handguns. He was deadly with his rifle but he had left it behind at the Caldwell house. He thought of taking it. The reason he hadn't was because it was awkward, the boot he'd gotten from the liveryman was for a carbine, his rifle-stock stood up out of the boot almost a foot and a half.

There was another consideration: He did not want to meet Coombs and Roberts looking like someone seeking a fight. This meeting, if it occurred was going to be hard enough to bring off, he didn't want anything to arouse the renegades.

Coombs and Roberts intended to ride as far as was necessary to study the area where the meeting was to occur. Their difficulty was with Lottie, the youngest, she cried often and was restless. They hadn't tied either child; where they had taken them into the uplands, blindfolded with soiled old bandanas was too far for a child, or even an adult, to walk back. The blindfolds had effectively disoriented each child. It had been Coombs' idea, it was doubtful if Roberts would have thought of blindfolds.

Lottie got on the men's nerves. If she wasn't crying she pleaded with Coombs and Roberts, or wandered restlessly.

Once Roberts flared up at the oldest girl. "Settle that danged kid down."

Sarah flared back. "She's hungry and frightened."

"Well; feed her some jerky then, but get her to settle down," Roberts growled.

Coombs was sitting with his back to a huge red fir tree. When he spoke it wasn't to the girls, it was to his partner. He sounded half amused. "Now you know what it'd be like to have a family, Jack."

Roberts wasn't in the mood. He flared back at Dan Coombs. "A family? I never seen a female woman I'd marry. They ain't for marryin'. As for kids, I can't stand 'em."

Coombs arose without haste, dusted

off and jerked his head. "It's time. The sod-buster'll likely be there."

"Maybe not," growled out-of-sorts Jack Roberts.

"He'll be there. Anyone who coddles his kids will be waitin'. You mind 'em until I get back."

Roberts faced his partner. He was tall but not as compactly and powerfully put together. "We go together. That's how we figured it. You go down there by yourself and chances are that squatter will try to bushwhack you."

Coombs remained calm. "That's exactly what he won't do if only one of us shows up. He can be a dumb squatter but if one of us stays with the children he'll know tryin' to bushwhack me will ruin his chances of ever finding his girls."

Roberts remained angrily stiff, but the longer he said nothing the more what Coombs had said made sense. He relaxed. "Bring back four thousand dollars," he grumbled and watched Coombs saddle up and start down out of the uplands.

Sarah asked where Coombs was going and disgruntled Jack Roberts replied sharply. "To get some money from your paw so's we can get rid of you . . . Is that damned kid crying again?"

"I told you, we're hungry, and Lottie's afraid. She cried in her sleep last night."

Roberts got jerky from a saddlebag, gave each child several sticks, and when they became quiet he stalked among the trees and did not return for fifteen minutes. They were still chewing. Dried jerky not only required a lot of chewing, but the more it was chewed the larger each mouthful became. It was nourishing, it was also salty, water helped fill stomachs. The combination gave an illusion of being replete, but as a steady diet it encouraged cravings for other food.

Children sometimes made out better with jerky than men did. Lottie finished her jerky, went to a rumpled blanket in tree shade, curled up and slept.

Roberts watched, shook his head and sighed. Sarah was not sleepy. She asked when they could go back to that town.

Roberts' mood had improved. "Maybe tomorrow. It depends on your paw." Roberts looked at the eight-year-old. You'll have a story to tell your kids, won't you?"

Sarah nodded and gazed at the lanky renegade without answering. She said something that startled Roberts. "Do you know my grandpaw?"

Roberts did not reply for a moment, then shook his head. "No. Who is he?"

"Sam Croft. He owns a big ranch. He's not going to like what you did."

Roberts smiled but did not speak. By the time their grandpaw figured things out he and Coombs would be so far out of the territory Sam Croft or the Angel Gabriel would never go as far as men could get, take different names and live good.

106

Sarah had another question. "What is your name?"

Roberts' smile lingered. "John Smith. What's yours?"

"Sarah Caldwell."

Roberts' smile vanished. "That preacher's kin to you?"

"No. It just happens our names are the same. Mister Smith, how did you know where Lottie and I were?"

Roberts studied Sarah. For a spindly kid she was coyote. He did not like children, they whined and got in the way, but Sarah was not afraid of him. She spoke up and talked back. He squared around slightly so that they were facing each other. "I guess it won't hurt to tell you. Me'n my partner — whose name is Dan Jones — we scouted up the town. It wasn't hard. We knew your paw had four kids with him in the wagon. We'd heard some talk about the preacher havin' taken in four kids no one knew . . . We seen you leave the preacher's house, shagged you, caught you out and grabbed you."

"You might have gotten the wrong kids, Mister Smith."

Roberts was beginning to enjoy this conversation. It beat hell out of squirming until Dan got back. Roberts was by nature an impatient man. He hated waiting. It was part of his hair-triggered nature, his inherent flightiness.

His slight smile returned. "But we didn't get the wrong kids, did we?"

Sarah changed the subject. "When will Mister Jones come back?"

Roberts' smile vanished again. "It's a long ride down where he went. Maybe tonight, otherwise in the morning." Roberts couldn't resist the urge to frighten Sarah. "What's the matter, don't you like our company?"

She answered while looking him in the eye. "No."

Roberts arose, turned his back on Sarah and went into forest shade not far from where Lottie was sleeping. His dawning interest in Sarah had turned swiftly to annoyance by her answer.

Heat came, not directly because of the forest canopy, but heat nonetheless. Sarah went to the creek, drank her fill and returned. Roberts watched her. He had a feeling Sarah would try to run away; she was something bizarre in his experience with females. Seemingly unafraid and independent as a hog on ice.

Sarah returned to her blanket, curled onto her side and slept. Roberts went to a clearing to find his horse. It was asleep in its hobbles, standing hip-shot, full as a tick of mountain meadow graze.

He returned to the camp, sat and leaned against an old-growth fir tree with scratch marks on it where a bear had torn bark off in its search for grubs.

He tipped his hat, thought of what he would do with his share of the four thousand dollars and slept.

He was awakened when something cold brushed his cheek. Sarah was standing beside him with Roberts' six-gun in both hands. He became clear-headed in a moment. The child said, "Mister Smith I want to go back to that town."

He sat perfectly still, she was very close, too close in fact for someone who had not cocked the Colt. Roberts was, like most edgy people, very fast. He struck out, hard. Sarah lost the gun. He struck again. Sarah went backwards and rolled. She arose dazed with a trickle of blood flung back on one cheek.

Roberts was on his feet holstering the gun as he said, "I ought to kill you, you little bitch."

Sarah held a hand to her mouth, tasted blood, lowered the hand, saw blood. She was still dazed by the blow. Without a word she went back to her blanket, sank to both knees and cried.

Roberts looked at Lottie. She was still asleep. He growled for Sarah to shut up. He could handle Sarah, who was older, but Lottie, who cried a lot, left him feeling exasperated and helpless.

Sarah choked back her sobs, kept her small back to the renegade, and fought hard to stifle her cries. She succeeded so well she developed hiccups.

Roberts swore. "Oh, fer Chris'sake. I'm beginning to wonder if four thousand dollars is worth this." He glanced at the sun, which was well on its way down the westerly sky, spat in disgust and resumed his position sitting against the fir tree. This time he put his six-gun in his lap with both hands atop it.

They had never tied the girls. They were confident they wouldn't try to wander off in a forest where cougars, bears, even wolves lived. They were also confident the children would not know which way to go if they thought of escaping, and finally, little Lottie wouldn't have the stamina for an attempt at escape. She was little more than a baby.

As the day wore along Roberts

grudgingly fed the girls, was relieved that Lottie ate then napped again. He and Sarah, who had washed the blood off her cheek, which was slightly swollen, had a new relationship. Sarah would not speak nor even look at Roberts. She did not eat much either.

With evening shadows subtly coming into the highlands, Roberts began to worry even though he knew Coombs could not make the ride to the pine tree and back in daylight. He would most likely find a hiding place to bed down tonight and arrive in the morning — with their riches.

A terrible thought occurred to Roberts. Four thousand dollars was more money than he or his partner could imagine. It would be a hell of a temptation to anyone, partners or not. What would he do if Coombs had gotten the money and had kept on riding?

Hunt the son of a bitch down if it took the rest of his life. And the girls? Hell with them, let the bears and wolves have them.

He worked himself into a calculating fury, but violent emotions do not endure. After dusk had settled and he had made a small fire, he told himself Coombs would never do that. They had been partners too long. He and Coombs had trusted each other before. They had been in some bad situations and had fought their way clear as partners.

It almost worked and might have if Jack Roberts hadn't been flighty, suspicious, inherently distrustful, but with nightfall coming even finding his way back down out of the uplands in darkness would be difficult. He would wait until morning because he had to.

He did not think about Sarah and Lottie.

9

A Bad Time

JAKE had to bluff; he was desperate enough to make it believable. Otherwise, he knew with men like Coombs and Roberts bluffing might not work. Probably wouldn't. Men who would abduct children would be unlikely to talk; they would expect money.

He had no idea where the constable and Lynch Miller were hiding, and along toward mid-afternoon when he saw a solitary rider approaching it had not occurred to him that only one renegade would appear.

His heart sank as his mind raced. He should have anticipated this but hadn't. The oncoming horseman was riding at a walk. Jake could sense the man's wariness even without noticing

114

how he sat erect in the saddle, the tie-down thong off his six-gun, and his head occasionally turning as he scanned the area.

The huge old unkempt tree cast the only shade for several hundred yards. There was a scattering of large grey rocks not too distant behind Jake. He made a guess that was where Lynch and the constable would be. He also thought briefly it must be hotter than the hinges of hell among those rocks with no shade.

He had tied the livery horse, and until it scented or heard the approaching horse, it dozed. It became wide awake as Dan Coombs got closer, close enough to see Jake leaning against the big tree.

For Jake the fact that his girls were not with Coombs, and the fact that Roberts had evidently remained behind with them was not a surprise, but he had hoped very hard Sarah and Lottie would be with their abductor. It was an unrealistic expectation, which he understood as Coombs got close enough for Jake to see his face.

Again, if he had ever seen the man before he didn't remember it. Coombs hadn't shaved lately, his face was weathered-dark, his chin was firm, the lips a slash across the lower part of his face.

Jake sensed the man's toughness even before Coombs drew rein, rested both hands atop the saddlehorn and briefly sat gazing at Jake. He wasted no time nor did he raise his voice when he said, "You got the money?"

Jake countered Coombs' question with one of his own. "Where are my little girls?"

"You can have 'em when you give me four thousand dollars."

Jake straightened up off the tree. "Show me my children then we'll talk about the money."

Coombs looked up and around. "Are you alone, squatter?"

Jake nodded without speaking. Coombs returned his hard gaze to the taller man beside the big tree. "I come a long way . . . The money."

"When I see my daughters, Mister Coombs."

The use of his name seemed to momentarily surprise the renegade. He sat his saddle for a moment gazing steadily at Jake. Eventually he said, "Mister, I don't have all day."

To this point neither man had raised his voice. They could have been discussing the weather. Jake tried reason, knowing in advance it would fail. "You sure as hell didn't expect me to hand over four thousand dollars an' watch you ride away without seein' my little girls, did you?"

Coombs' horse was getting restless, most horses did when they were standing still being used for a chair. He growled at the animal and cast another searching gaze in all directions.

When he finally swung down he gazed at Jake's holstered six-gun. "You any good with that thing?" he asked, and Jake shrugged. "Most likely not as good as you are."

The renegade made a mirthless small smile. "As long as you know you ain't." Coombs paused looking steadily at Jake. Eventually he spoke again. "All right, squatter; show me the money if you got it. Then I'll fetch one girl, keep the other'n back until you give us the money."

Coombs, having never tried abduction, was as green at it as Jake was. He hadn't expected what was happening, but he was able to understand Jake's position. "Let's get this over with," he said in a slightly annoyed voice. "Now I got to go back empty-handed, an' my partner's not goin' to like that. Show me the money an' I'll go back and fetch the little one down here an' you'll pay in full, or you might not see the other one."

Coombs was clearly disappointed. He was also irritated; it had been a long ride down here, and now he would have to make the same ride back without four thousand dollars. If he ever tried this again he would know how to do it better. Meanwhile his irritation was increasing. "Show me the damned money, or ain't you got it?"

A horseman appeared out of the nearby rocks riding slack and on loose reins. He called a greeting to the two men by the tree. It was Lynch Miller slouching along as though he didn't have a worry in the world.

Coombs tensed, lips pulled flat, right hand within inches of his holster. He spoke swiftly and softly: "Who is he?"

Jake lied with a straight face. "I got no idea. Maybe a drifter."

Coombs moved slightly away so that he had both men in view. His right hand still hovered.

Lynch called again. "You boys seen any cattle over here? I ride for the feller who's shy about thirty head an' his best bull."

Lynch was an excellent actor, he let his reins swing, continued to sit loose, and he smiled. Jake was no less surprised than Dan Coombs was, but the renegade seemed to loosen slightly as Jake called back. "Nope. Haven't even seen any cattle tracks."

Lynch stopped far enough away, not wanting to take a chance on being recognised by Coombs, swung off with one rein in his hand and swore. "The old man I work for said that damned bull always comes over in this direction lookin' for bulling cows. They got enough down in Coldwater an' the old bull's got a memory like a calendar."

Jake shook his head. "Didn't you track 'em?" he asked and Lynch swore again. "No. The old man said I'd find him over here more'n likely with as many cows an' heifers as he could herd along. I didn't look for sign, I figured the old man knew his bull so I took a short cut."

Lynch was briefly silent. He did not pay much attention to Coombs. Jake had been the one who had spoken to him. Without another curse he swung back into the saddle and spoke as he was turning in the direction of Coldwater.

"It's gettin' too damned hot for scourin' around for cattle." He nodded to the men on the ground. "As long as I'm this close to town I might as well get some beer."

Lynch rode southward as he had ridden before, slouched, relaxed, reins swinging. Coombs was no longer tense, but he seemed unwilling to linger much longer. He gathered his reins, swung into the saddle and in a growly tone of voice said, "Tomorrow, squatter. I'll bring the one that cries all the time, the littlest one, and you be here an' hand over the money."

Coombs rode back northward sitting twisted in the saddle. He doubted Jake would shoot him in the back, under the circumstances that would really endanger his children, but Dan Coombs hadn't lived this long by being careless. He continued to ride like that until he was out of hand-gun range.

121

Then he boosted his horse over into a lope and held him to it until he was nearly out of sight.

Down the road about two miles Lynch and Constable Denton Wright were sitting in shade provided by a lowering sun, horses dozing, patiently waiting.

When Jake rode up they arose and dusted off. Lynch spoke first. "He came alone. From that we figured his partner was somewhere with the children. We could have shot him any time — he was a sitting duck. You can guess why we didn't; it'd leave your little girls with the other one."

Jake dismounted. The three of them talked for about fifteen minutes. What worried Jake most was that when Coombs returned with Lottie, he would still be unable to pay the ransom, and Coombs would never in gawd's green world, be put off again.

On the ride back to Coldwater Jake and the constable talked, Lynch was thoughtfully quiet, which Jake accepted, he had known Lynch Miller a long time and had noticed that Lynch had never been a really talkative individual.

There were people at the minister's house. When the three horsemen tied up out front scarcely a word was spoken. Jake related his experience and its result.

There was not a whole lot of conversation afterwards. Except for one or two women, the small crowd was mostly quiet. As with Lynch the men seemed thoughtfully quiet.

The minister's wife went into the kitchen to be alone, and cried. Anna Croft followed her, took Fannie in her arms to soothe her.

Several men slapped Jake lightly on the shoulder as the small crowd left the house. Lynch went as far as the tie-rack with the others, untied the three horses and led them down to the livery barn. The hostler down there was full of questions. Lynch answered a couple and smiled in silence about the others.

What was left of the day townspeople spent sombrely. They were by this time as upset as Jake was. The men at the saloon unanimously agreed the renegades who had stolen Jake's little girls deserved hanging.

When the evening stage arrived the driver, a muscular man with a reddish tint to his full beard, added something to the abduction story. As he was coming out of the highlands for the steady lone run to Coldwater, he had seen a solitary rider a short distance on the west side of the road riding into the upland country.

Several townsmen asked for an estimate of when the whip had seen that horseman, then roughly worked it out that the time lapse was right for the horseman to be Coombs, and since there had been almost no traffic in that area, it had to be the man townsmen unanimously wanted to hang.

But the mountains were vast, miles deep and many more miles wide. Someone suggested making up a posse, spreading far apart and making a sweep. The idea was quickly, scornfully killed. Even if the noise of a posse coming didn't alert the renegades, if the abductors only indifferently kept watch, posse riders would be seen.

Along toward late afternoon, with the entire town with just one thing on its mind, the saloonman had a noticeable drop in customers, as did the proprietor of the general store.

No one had ever had anything like this happen to them before, they were absorbed by it. If the stolen human beings had been adults it might have been different, but they were children, one child just barely four years old.

Every woman in Coldwater, those with children of their own and those without, were equally, or even more, incensed than the men.

Constable Wright was fearful some scatterbrained hot-head would head into the mountains on his own, and they might have except with the advent of dusk with darkness to follow, locating

Coombs and Roberts in the dark would result, in the least, of someone being heard and ambushed.

At the preacher's house Jake picked at his supper. Tomorrow couldn't help but end in disaster. He closed his mind to what the renegades might do to his little girls when Jake tried to bargain, offering fifteen hundred dollars rather than the full amount, which the abductors were by now certainly anticipating.

Fannie left the supper table in mid-meal, went to her bedroom and cried. Anna would have gone to her but the preacher shook his head.

William and Joseph, infected with the gloom of their elders, were as quiet as mice, ate with their heads down and escaped from the table as soon as they could.

Lynch re-filled coffee cups without speaking, his face a mask. Anna didn't finish her meal. She arose to begin scooping up dishes to be washed. With her back to the others she became busy cleaning up. Before the others left the table she came forward with a damp cloth and began vigorously scrubbing the tabletop. She did not look into the faces. She was as near to tears as she had ever been without actually shedding them. Her jaws were locked in a fight to retain self-control.

The reverend caught Anna's attention with a question. "Ma'am; would your husband have that much money by any chance?"

Anna stopped swabbing the table. Her reply was given without facing the minister. "My husband was out with the riders making a gather when Lynch and I left . . . Reverend Caldwell, my husband has had nothing to do with my daughter and her husband since they got married."

It wasn't an answer to the preacher's question but it left no doubt in the minds of the others at the table who didn't already know it, that Anna's husband was an unrelenting individual.

They bedded down dreading the

arrival of dawn. Reverend Caldwell had crisscrossed the town, asking, pleading, and while the townsfolk had given generously as they could all he had collected was seventeen hundred and eighty-five dollars and sixty cents.

In the morning Lynch went down to the livery barn before the others were up. Had a brief discussion with the liveryman and returned as Anna and Fannie were preparing breakfast in silence.

It was another sombre meal. Jake, whose desperation had not let him sleep well, had made a decision he did not share with the others. He would use his six-gun today. The plan was very simple. He would throw-down on Coombs, get Lottie, then force Coombs to lead him to the hide-out. It was a simple plan but not a very wise one. Roberts would see or hear Coombs returning with Sarah's father, and Jake had to have known Roberts was good with guns. Desperate people are rarely rational. Jake wasn't.

Constable Wright arrived at the minister's house shortly after breakfast. He took Jake and Lynch aside. What he had to say did not take long. "Mister Miller an' I'll head out like we done before. I know it's daylight, but yestiddy he didn't come along until after noon. We'll get into them rocks, and when he hands over your little girl, we'll take him. Not shoot the bastard, just come out of the rocks ready to if he gets troublesome."

Jake was frowning. Before he could protest the constable also said, "I figure this is a boot that fits both feet. We'll take him alive an' trade him for your oldest girl."

Lynch looked sceptical. "How do we get word to the other one about the trade? We got no idea where they're hid out."

The constable replied shortly. "Coombs will tell us how to find the camp if I got to half skin him alive."

It was a dangerous notion, but Jake saw it as a possible solution, and even though it hinged on there not being a gunfight, maybe with Coombs getting killed which meant they would not find the hide-out, it was better than his plan; at least the odds would be three-to-one, and unless Coombs was very fast and deadly with his shooting iron, it just might work.

Lynch said nothing. He stood looking at the ground wearing a slight frown which Jake and the constable took to mean he was worried about the chance of success. That was not what Lynch was faintly frowning about at all.

Lynch left with the constable to get their animals and leave town, Jake went back inside, said nothing, got his shellbelt and six-gun from the bedroom, buckled them into place and left the house without a word to anyone.

Reverend Caldwell scratched his head. Clearly, the constable, Jake and the Croft ranch rider were up to something. He hadn't asked; none of the trio seemed willing to take him into their confidence, which did not bother him as a slight, but which *did* bother him otherwise.

It was a beautiful morning, more like spring than mid-summer. Jake got the same roan horse from the liveryman, who did not say ten words to Jake, and who walked up to the front of his runway to watch Jake ride toward the north end of town, before going over to the cafe for breakfast.

Jake rode without haste, Coombs would not arrive for several hours, if he made the ride as he had yesterday. Jake could not have loafed around town. He wanted Lottie; he wanted to get this over with.

People saw Jake riding north. This was to be another day when townsfolk had to wait with their fears. Even those who did not know Coombs had given Jake an ultimatum which was to be resolved today, they assumed correctly that was the situation.

Coldwater was quieter than it had been in a long time. Occasionally small communities could be brought together by events. This event involved two children, one four and one eight.

Jake reached the big old pine tree while the morning was still cool. There was no sign of Lynch or the constable, but he had seen tracks where two riders had left the road about a mile back.

The land in all directions was highlighted by the rising sun, and it was empty. Jake studied the distant mountains before a heat-haze made them less than distinct. There was no rider coming from the north.

He lifted out his six-gun, carefully examined it, tested his draw several times, put up the gun and wagged his head. In a shoot-out he was not going to win against Dan Coombs, he felt certain of that. A shoot-out was not something he wanted; regardless of who got killed, Sarah would still be somewhere in the mountains.

Later, when a bird sounded from the direction of the rocks, the constable stood head and shoulders above a large boulder gesturing.

Jake had been too preoccupied with his thoughts to be watching. The constable pointed with a rigid arm. A solitary horseman was coming from the north. Even at that distance it could be seen he was not alone in the saddle.

It was past mid-day, the benign early morning had turned into an increasingly hot afternoon.

Jake lifted his six-gun and dropped it back into its holster several times, and was only marginally faster the last time than he had been the first time.

He was sweating in tree-shade. Even if he'd practised with the gun in his spare time, he doubted he could survive against a man who lived by the gun.

He had the wad of money Reverend Caldwell had given him last night, in a shirt pocket. He had folded it over which made it seem like much more money than it was, but he had no illusions; when he handed Coombs the money in exchange for Lottie, the renegade would surely at least finger through it.

He was counting on this part of his plan, which was to give Coombs the money for Lottie, which was roughly half what the renegade expected, and tell him he could have the other half when he brought Sarah back. He knew the renegade would expect the entire four thousand dollars; that's what their discussion yesterday had implied. He had no doubt that Coombs would be disappointed and therefore angry. He might view Jake's action as betrayal.

10

Anna's Surprise

COOMBS rode as warily as he had the other time, which was unnecessary since he was holding little Lottie in front of him on the saddle, but outlaw instincts were ingrained.

Lottie saw her father step from the shelter of the big old tree. She squealed and squirmed. Coombs gave her a rough yank and ordered her to be quiet.

She became quiet and stopped squirming, but as the pair rode closer Jake could see her unnaturally rigid body in the saddle.

Coombs drew rein in tree shade. This time when Lottie struggled against his arm, he let her down. She ran forward where Jake knelt to hold her.

She cried and clung to her father as Jake arose.

Coombs, evidently unaffected by this interlude, sat his saddle as he said, "The money, squatter."

Jake removed the wad of folded notes from his shirt pocket. When Coombs swung down Jake said, "Half, Mister Coombs. The other half when you give me my other girl."

Coombs stopped a few feet ahead of his horse looking steadily at Jake, who was holding out the folded bundle of money. Now, Jake told himself, there will be trouble. With Lottie clinging to his leg he braced to draw. For the first time in his life he felt totally inadequate. They were no more than twenty feet apart. Neither man could miss at that distance, and if Coombs was faster, the child clinging to his leg and her sister would be orphans.

He knew Lynch and the constable were watching. Coombs eyed that folded bundle of money and asked how much there was.

Jake answered quietly. "Seventeen hundred dollars."

"It looks like more," the renegade said in a calm, almost musing tone of voice.

"Take it and count it," Jake replied, beginning to wonder where the anger he had expected had gone. It was the sight of the folded, thick wad of greenbacks, something Dan Coombs probably had never seen in such quantities before. He took the money, fingered through it without more than glancing at what he was doing, his attention still on the homesteader in front of him wearing a sidearm. He said, "Mister, if you're lyin' you'll never see the other one."

"I'm not lying. Count it. It's almost half what I agreed to pay for their return."

Coombs seemed inclined to count the money. He was also aware that the longer he stood there the greater the chance of someone coming up the road.

He put the folded bills in a shirt

pocket, buttoned the pocket and said, "Squatter. That wasn't the trade. You was supposed to have the full four thousand."

Coombs sounded more argumentative than angry, which emboldened Jake. "Maybe, Mister Coombs, but I had all night to figure this was the only way I'd be sure I'd get both my children."

Coombs, with a fortune in a shirt pocket, stood briefly considering Jake, then turned, swung back into the saddle and said, "Tomorrow," and rode northward in the same direction he had ridden the day before, and in the same way, sitting sideways looking back until he was beyond pistol range.

Jake picked Lottie up, mounted the roan horse and started toward town. She was quiet and limp in his arms. Once she kissed his cheek and he in return kissed the side of her head where it rested on his shoulder. Neither one of them said a word until they met Lynch and Denton Wright two miles farther along waiting in the shade of the same tree where they had been the day before.

When her father halted Lottie looked around. She knew Lynch but the lanky constable was a stranger. She tightened her grip around Jake's neck.

He laughed softly, told her the stranger was a friend, swung to the ground holding Lottie and introduced her to the constable. His easy and genuine smile and offer of a very large hand made a good enough impression on the child for her to put out her small hand.

Lynch winked. Lottie, who had recently learned how to wink, winked back.

Jake told them of the experience back yonder. They seemed relieved until Lynch said, "Tomorrow? There ain't no more money, Jake."

Jake nodded; he knew that, in fact he had thought of little else after getting his youngest child back. They did as they'd done before, rode on a loose rein back to Coldwater, mostly silent.

Lottie fell asleep in her father's arms. She was exhausted, tired and dirty.

When they arrived in town people in doorways, on the plankwalks, in the street called congratulations. At the preacher's house when the child saw her grandmother she ran into her arms. Fannie looked over Anna's head at Jake with arched eyebrows. Lynch answered the unasked question. "Tomorrow he'll bring the other one. He took the money as half payment."

Except for the murmurings of Anna Croft and her grandchild the room was silent. Fannie Caldwell sank into a chair. She muttered, "Tomorrow . . ?"

No one answered her but within moments her husband arrived home from the general store, and amid fresh rejoicing no one remembered what she had said.

They didn't need a reminder. The rejoicing over the recovery of Lottie was tempered by the dilemma yet to come.

Fannie and Anna Croft took Lottie

into the kitchen to be fed. Later they would bathe her and re-dress her in some of Fannie's daughter's clothes saved from when the daughter had been Lottie's size. Too much had happened, Lottie fell into a sound sleep on Fannie Caldwell's bed. The women returned to the parlour but the men were gone.

They hadn't gone far, Lynch would have liked a double whiskey but said nothing; Reverend Caldwell might have approved but it was doubtful that he would have accompanied them to the saloon.

Several townsmen joined them at the livery barn where the taciturn, burly proprietor listened a lot but said little. He said something to Lynch when the two men were slightly apart from the others. Lynch didn't answer, he simply shrugged his shoulders.

It was along toward evening when the minister and Jake were sitting sombrely in the parlour waiting to be summoned to supper, when a heavy fist hammered on the front door.

The preacher went to open it. He did not know the grizzled, dusty man standing there as he asked if this was the residence of Reverend Caldwell. Behind him he heard Jake spring from his chair. Lynch did not move.

The travel-stained forceful-appearing man in the doorway introduced himself to Reverend Caldwell in a steely voice. "I'm Sam Croft. I understand that my wife is here."

Caldwell stepped aside. Sam Croft walked inside, saw Jake, saw Lynch looking straight back, and true to his direct nature addressed Lynch. "How much did you pay the skinny lad on the runnin' horse to come for me?"

Lynch answered without arising. "Three dollars. The liveryman let him have the running mare."

Sam bobbed his head. "I owe you, Lynch. The liveryman told me what's happened so far."

Up to this point Sam Croft had

hardly more than glanced at his son-in-law, but now he did. "Jake, where are the children?"

"William and Joseph are getting ready for supper. Lottie's asleep."

"Where is Sarah?"

"They still have her."

Sam Croft did not say it loudly enough for the women in the kitchen to hear him, but there was venom in the words. "Those double-crossing sons of bitches. Where are they?"

"Back in the mountains somewhere," Jake replied, and explained how he had gotten Lottie, and what the problem was in getting Sarah back. "All the money folks here could spare was seventeen hundred dollars. I gave that to Coombs this afternoon for Lottie."

"And?"

"Tomorrow he'll fetch Sarah expecting the rest of the money — which we don't have."

Sam said, "Where is Anna?"

"In the kitchen."

Sam did not ask the direction of the

kitchen, he didn't have to, the aroma of supper being prepared directed him. He pushed open the door, Anna looked and gasped. Croft shook his head at her. He then said something unexpected. "Anna, I'm not your enemy. I'm the best friend you have. I knew you were slipping over there to visit. Why in gawd's name didn't you tell me what Jake was planning?"

Anna recovered from the shock of seeing her husband and faced him when she replied. "Because I didn't know what he was planning. It was something between your daughter and her husband."

"Anna, you'n Lynch tracking him was foolish. I would have gone along an' taken the whole crew."

Anna spoke tartly. "You were making a gather, Sam. That's always come first with you."

Fannie Caldwell interrupted by introducing herself and inviting Sam Croft to stay for supper. He made a tight small smile of appreciation but he explained that he had engaged a room at the local boarding house.

He did not introduce himself, after the exchange between the stranger and Anna Croft it hadn't been necessary.

He and his wife exchanged a long look before Sam returned to the parlour where he regarded Lynch steadily for a moment, then smiled at him. Lynch had expected almost anything but this. He smiled back as he said, "I figured this was goin' to end up in either a Mexican stand-off or someone gettin' hurt. The folks here in Coldwater collected that seventeen hundred dollars Jake give Dan Coombs. I knew some days back there wouldn't ever be enough money, so I sent the rider for you." Lynch gently shook his head. "I didn't know what else to do."

Sam took a chair opposite Reverend Caldwell. "I owe you," he told the minister.

Reverend Caldwell had known many cowmen with Sam Croft's tough hard-driving personality. He replied quietly.

"You don't owe me anything, Mister Croft. I have a family too. A man's greatest responsibility is to his kin. I hope you'd do for me what I've done for yours'."

Sam sat leaning forward clasping both work-roughened hands, staring at the minister. He understood exactly the implication behind Caldwell's words.

Finally, he looked at his son-in-law. "I had Susan taken to town for the funeral."

Jake spoke coldly. "She wanted to be buried on the ranch."

"Did she tell you that?"

"Yes, shortly before she died."

Sam looked at his clasped hands for a moment before speaking again. "All right; that's where she'll be buried . . . Jake?"

"Yes."

"I have the money to get Sarah back. But I want Roberts and Coombs almost as bad."

Lynch dryly said, "So does everyone in Coldwater. You got any idea, Sam?

146

Jake's got to meet Coombs five miles north of town tomorrow."

Croft arose, went to a window and looked out as he spoke. "I'll give you the money, you give it to that son of a bitch. Is there a decent hidin' place out there?"

"Some big rocks where Lynch and the town constable hid."

"Did they sneak out there in the dark?"

"Not yesterday because Coombs didn't show up until noon or later. Where they got their camp it's got to be a long way into the mountains."

Sam reverted to a characteristic mood. "I don't care where their camp is. I just want to make damned sure nothin' goes wrong." He faced around looking at Lynch. "You willin' to go out there after dark tonight?"

Lynch nodded without speaking. Sam still looked at him as he asked about the town constable and Lynch nodded again, but he also said, "It's up to him but I'm sure he'll do it." After a brief moment he added a thought. "I got a feelin' both Coombs and Roberts will come. There won't be no reason for one of them to stay behind after they deliver Sarah an' get their money."

Sam Croft's eyes narrowed. "All the better if they do. I want those two by the heels whatever it takes. No one does what they did to my granddaughters. No one on the face of this earth!"

Sam Croft made the same impression on the residents of Coldwater as he made on others. It may have been intuitive, because although they understood his angry concern, they still withheld from Sam the compassion they felt for Jake, Anna and Lynch.

Anna Croft's long-suffering exasperation with her husband boiled over when Sam's shortness with people, his hard-driving personality, made her take Sam to the wood shed behind the Coldwell house. They were in serious trouble. She had been surprised that quiet Lynch Miller had sent for him. She was even more surprised when he appeared on the Caldwells' front porch. Her long-time acceptance that her husband would not change coupled to her anxiety for Sarah made her say things she might not otherwise have said.

Sam did not get a chance to speak until she had finished. "You," she told him, "are not making matters better you are making them worse. The folks of this town scraped up every dollar they could to help us. As long as we live we'll be indebted to them."

Sam started to speak, to tell Anna he would see that every person who donated would be re-paid. She cut him off before he could say a word. "Be quiet! I'm not through! Sam, it began when Jake and Susan fell in love. You rejected Jake before you even got to know him. He did his best for Susan and the children. She was happy with him Sam, I'm going to tell you something: After we get Sarah back and get back home, I'm going to pack up and leave."

After all their years of marriage Anna had finally had enough. Sam had no illusions that his wife meant what she said. He had not expected that last sentence and stood like a stone looking at her. Anna started briskly out of the wood-shed. Sam made no move to stop her, he simply stood like a stone watching her cross to the house and slam the door from the inside.

He didn't eat with the others, he went down to the cafe, where he was greeted with reserved nods and no words. Even the cafeman was cool toward him. He ordered his meal, ate it, and when he arose to put coins beside the plate he smiled at the cafeman and said, "That was a right good supper, friend."

A dozen sets of eyes followed his exit from the cafe. Nothing was said afterwards, townsmen ate in thoughtful silence. People weren't won over by one pleasant statement, but it was a beginning.

He went down to the livery barn,

asked the burly, nearly expressionless proprietor if he had Jake's wagon. The burly man nodded his head. Sam asked if he knew where it was. The liveryman said it was out back where he parked his own wagons. Sam smiled as he reached into a pocket and said, "For lookin after it an' its contents," and handed the liveryman three dollars.

The liveryman's eyes widened. A dollar would have been sufficient. He took the money, nodded and said, "It'll be here whenever your son-in-law wants it." He did not smile but relaxed his stiff stance. Sam gave him a pat on the shoulder and left.

The liveryman followed him up the runway as far as the road and watched him walking north. He felt a tinge of guilt for pre-judging a man on the gossipy talk of others, then gave his head a slight shake, looked at the money in his hand and wondered why folks had misjudged Sam Croft. It was another beginning and it hadn't actually been that hard for Sam.

He met Constable Wright, had a long talk with him during which Wright agreed to again accompany Lynch to the ambushing site that night. When they parted they shook hands. The constable had refused to take money for what he would do that night, but the offer, generous by any standard, had impressed him favourably. He too watched Sam walk away, but in easy-going Denton Wright's opinion, the murmurings around town hadn't really made much of an impression anyway. He knew his town and its residents. He had no trouble deciding Sam Croft was not what some folks hinted that he was, another overbearing cowman.

Lynch was out front on the preacher's porch sitting cocked-back on a cane-backed chair when Sam came up to the porch. He nodded without speaking. Sam nodded back, hesitated a moment before taking another chair to sit on as he addressed his tired rider. "I owe you," he said, for the second time.

Lynch barely inclined his head and did not speak.

"Seems you was the only one who knew what to do, an' did it."

Lynch looked around at his boss. "It didn't take much thinkin', Sam. These folks had dug up every dollar they had, there's no bank in Coldwater and Jake needed that extra money worse than he'd ever need it again — and you were the only person I knew who might have it."

Sam considered work-thickened hands in his lap as he replied. "But you *did* it, Lynch."

The hired rider shrugged slightly as though to dismiss a subject that was embarrassing. He also changed the course of their conversation by asking how the gather was coming along back home.

Sam smiled ruefully. "Well, we're about half through. With you'n me not there to help the boys'll be short-handed, but I'd say they'll about have it finished when we get back . . . Lynch?

With this whole town roused up, how'd you keep some damned fool from tryin' to find the girls?"

"I didn't, Sam. It was Jake and the constable who did that."

It wasn't entirely true but it was close enough and Lynch wanted to interject Jake's name into their palaver.

Sam continued to gaze at his hands. He hung-fire answering so long Lynch did not think he was going to do it, but he eventually did.

"Jake," he said slowly. "He shouldn't have run off like that."

Lynch took a long chance when he replied. "He did what he'd promised Susan."

"Yeah. So Anna told me. But . . ."

Lynch figured he was going to be fired anyway, so he did what Sam's wife had done. He let Sam have both barrels. "It don't matter whether you like Jake or not, but he's your son-in-law and those are his kids. My guess is that with Susan gone you'd take 'em from him . . . Sam, it wasn't Jake got everyone into this mess ... It was you."

Lynch's chair came down off the wall, he arose and went into the house. He didn't want to hear whatever Sam Croft would say. In fact Sam would have said nothing, as with Anna at the wood-shed he was too surprised by his hired hand's frankness to say anything.

11

Failure!

LATER, Sam caught Jake bringing in an arm load of firewood. They met at the wood shed. Sam handed Jake a folded wad of money. He also said, "Be careful. I don't want to raise those kids by myself." He stood there waiting for Jake to say something. Jake, with one arm holding the wood, took the money with his free hand as he regarded the older man. As he pocketed the money he said. "I'll be careful . . . Sam, I'll pay you back. Thanks."

Croft's answer surprised Jake. "No; you don't have to pay me back. Those kids are yours first, but they're my grandchildren . . . Remember what I said. Be careful."

Sam walked toward the house. Jake

did too but not until he had stood watching the other man. That hadn't been the Sam Croft he knew.

When darkness arrived Sam rounded up the constable and Lynch. They told him there was plenty of time. He would have argued but Anna was staring at him. He said, "All right; you lads done this before. I'd as leave take a nap. I'm plumb tired. I'm not as young as I once was."

He went into the parlour, stretched out on a couch and within moments was asleep. As he slept he had no idea Anna tiptoed in and stood gazing at him before she went back to the kitchen. She was silent for a long time.

Constable Wright come for Lynch and Sam in the wee hours. It was chilly. The lawman was bundled into a coat, Lynch and Sam followed his example before going for their horses. Each had a weapon slung forward under their saddle fenders as they left a sleeping town. The liveryman, who had been roused from his cot in the harness room, was even less talkative than he usually was.

It was not only cold it was also dark. The moon, which had been increasing in size for several days, cast weak light earthward.

They rode pretty much in silence. Each suspected it would be a long wait. Each of them would have felt better if they hadn't had to make this ride, not entirely because it was cold and they would have preferred sleeping, but also because, despite their thoughtful planning, the day yet to come might very well be their last if something went wrong, and with men like Coombs and Roberts it was impossible to make an accurate prediction.

In that respect they were right.

Day was breaking when they saw Jake on the roan horse. He was riding at a plodding walk. Once or twice he looked in the direction of the rocks. He knew they were in place because he had seen where they had veered away from the road, but he acted as though he did not know.

He tied the roan horse, which promptly went to sleep with most of its weight on three legs while Jake leaned on the big tree wrapped in an old blanket-coat. It would be a long wait, but he was reconciled to that; he would have waited much longer to get his eldest daughter back.

Surprisingly, as daylight improved and visibility got much better, he saw two riders coming on a southeasterly course. They would have been invisible a couple of hours earlier when the dark, bulky mountains would have backgrounded them. They might also have been invisible if the air hadn't been as clear as glass.

A bird-call came faintly from among the rearward large boulders. Jake did not even turn, but he raised an arm to signify he had also seen the riders. He did not think of his father-in-law who was notoriously one of the hell-for-leather individuals who did not wait for trouble to come to him; he charged headlong to face it.

The riders were in no hurry. It was a long time before Jake and the ambushers could make out Sarah riding double with Dan Coombs, behind the saddle.

The sun was well along on its overhead climb. The chill was gone but it was not hot yet, it was pleasantly warm. Jake shed his old coat, did as he'd done before, hoisted his six-gun, examined it, sank it back into its holster, drew several times to practice and, as before demonstrated that he was not a gunman and never would be. A dead-shot rifleman who was unaccustomed to hand-guns, at close range in a situation Jake was going to face, was as useless as teats on a boar.

The riders came ahead without haste. Coombs concentrated on the tree. He saw the dozing roan horse, was satisfied Jake was down there, but Jack Roberts had been getting nervous the closer they got. It was his nature, he was flighty. Once Jake saw him lean to say something to Dan Coombs, whose attention was on the roan horse and the big tree, seemed not to have heard or, if he did, not to have heeded whatever his partner had said.

But evidently he had heeded, because some distance out, he halted. Sarah was put on the ground, the two men briefly conferred before Coombs started riding ahead leaving Sarah and Roberts far enough behind to be out of hand-gun range.

Sam Croft in his rocky concealment said, "Son of a bitch!" Neither the constable nor Lynch moved nor made a sound. Evidently, rank amateurs though the renegades were they were not that rank. Instinct had warned them; as long as they had Sarah, her father would not be troublesome. Although both renegades held squatters in contempt, as did most range stockmen, gunshots could be heard down in town.

Jake stepped clear of the tree facing the

oncoming horseman. Coombs watched him like a hawk, ignoring everything but the man by the tree.

Coombs had a fair start on a beard. He either did not carry a razor in his saddlebags as most rangemen did who expected not to be near a town, or he didn't care about his appearance, more likely the latter.

He drew rein, put both hands atop the saddlehorn and looked at Jake for a moment before he said, "You got it?"

Jake took the folded money from his pocket and with Coombs looking on, forced it into the low crotch of the tree. He did this without speaking.

Coombs said, "Count it for me, squatter."

Jake's reply was short. "Count it yourself. It's all there. You asked for four thousand dollars, countin' what you got yesterday, this money totals four thousand."

Coombs shifted his attention from Jake to the surrounding countryside, and back. "Hand it up to me," he ordered.

Jake's reply was short again. "When you tell your partner to let my little girl come down here."

Coombs was facing a different man; he sensed it from Jake's tone of voice. He sat slouched in the saddle and once more scanned the empty-appearing countryside.

He kneed his horse closer, leaned from the saddle for the money. He was a lifelong horseman, reins in the left hand. His right arm was extended when a horse nickered over in the rocks. Jake beat Coombs to the draw before the renegade could pull back his extended arm. Not by much, but by enough for the renegade to freeze with his six-gun half drawn when Jake cocked his gun.

"Drop it," Jake said.

Coombs hesitated, but eventually let the six-gun fall. As he did this he said, "You damned fool. You'll never see your kid again . . . Who's hid in them rocks?"

Jake gave another order without answering the question. "Get down!"

Again the renegade was slow to obey, but he came down slowly facing Jake as he did so. He spoke again. "Roberts will blow her head off'

Jake was tempted to shoot Coombs. He would have if Sarah had not been out there with Roberts, watching the men by the tree.

Jake had his prisoner but that did not help his daughter. He told Coombs to signal Roberts to let Sarah walk toward the tree. Coombs obeyed with a high-flung gesture of one arm.

What happened was not what Jake expected. Roberts hauled Jake's daughter up behind the saddle and began riding toward the tree. He would see Jake's cocked six-gun long before he got there, and Jack Roberts was a hair-triggered individual. Coombs was looking straight at Jake, smiling. His lips were pulled back, his eyes were fixed on his captor. "You're goin' to get your little girl shot, squatter. No matter what happens she's goin' to get killed . . . Jack's no fool."

Jake's command of the situation might only be temporary. He almost regretted getting the drop on Coombs. He, Lynch and the constable had discussed most of the possibilities, but not the present one.

Sam Croft, who had ridden his fastest horse to reach Coldwater, which was a mare, was crouching some distance from where the horses were concealed when the mare either saw Roberts coming or caught the scent of another horse, and whinnied.

Everything changed in an instant. Roberts halted while he was still some distance away. He could see Jake's roan and his partner's bay. Neither of them had even looked around when they picked up the scent of Roberts' animal. They were geldings.

Roberts sat motionless for a long moment, then called ahead. "Dan; who's down there?"

Coombs faced Jake still wearing the

cold, bleak small smile. He made no attempt to answer his partner. Jake told him to yell back but Coombs stood like a stone, wearing the bleak smile. He made no move to obey.

Coombs was no longer the main player, his partner was, and whether Roberts was clever or not, he had been an outlaw long enough to function warily in everything he did. Right now, although he had not placed the location of Sam Croft's mare, he could see two horses and neither of them had made that noise.

Once more he called to Coombs. "Is it all right? Is something wrong?"

Again, Coombs faced Jake without moving or calling back.

Roberts reacted. He swung his horse and boosted it over into a hard run back the way it had come. Sarah was clinging to him as hard as she could, unaware that although she and Roberts were in carbine range, the men in the rocks could not fire; she was protecting her abductor's back.

The only sound for several moments was the echo of Roberts' running horse, then Coombs addressed Jake again. "You killed your own kid, squatter."

Jake's finger tightened slightly inside the trigger guard at the same moment three riders broke away from the big rocks riding in fast pursuit. Two of those animals were average, the third one began widening the distance within minutes. Sam Croft was riding the fastest animal.

Coombs picked a bad moment to dive for his six-gun. Jake saw him crouch to drop for the gun and squeezed the trigger. He had aimed for the renegade's mid-body. His bullet was a foot high. It struck Coombs in his off-side upper shoulder. Impact knocked Coombs sideways, too far from his weapon even if he'd tried to reach it. He hit the ground and rolled. The pain was enough to keep him down and writhing. Blood darkened his shirt up high. Pain kept him writhing. Each time he rolled the dust turned bright red.

Jake wanted to watch the horse race. It was miles to the mountains, Roberts was carrying double, and he had already ridden a long way out of the mountains to get down here.

Sam was gaining on him. Lynch and the constable were doing their best but the distance steadily widened.

Coombs' teeth-grinding noise diverted Jake's attention to the wounded man. He had wanted to kill the renegade but hadn't.

He picked up the wounded man's six-gun and shoved it under his belt, mounted the roan horse and flung away to join the pursuit.

The roan was no faster than average but it gave all it had. He did not even gain on Lynch or the constable. Roberts was still riding hard, but as Jake watched his mount seemed to be going up and down but not increasing its lead. Sam Croft's horse was rapidly closing on him. The foothills were not very distant. Sam evidently wanted to overtake the renegade before he got into the timber, which would be Roberts' only salvation — if he could get that far on an animal that was clearly giving out.

The heat did not help. With the sun almost directly overhead, in this kind of a situation any horse being pushed to its absolute limit, carrying double and having already been ridden many miles, would founder if he was kept at the pace Roberts was pushing the animal.

Once Roberts twisted in the saddle and fired his six-gun at Sam Croft who was finally within handgun range, but the hurricane back of a running horse was the worst of all places to shoot at someone.

Sam did not even flinch, nor did he fire back. He couldn't.

Lynch and Constable Wright began gaining on Roberts, whose horse was fast failing. He made it into the low foothills, flung off the spent animal which stood head hung sucking air, on the verge of being chest-foundered.

Another mile and he would have been.

Roberts yanked Sarah with him by the arm. She was too frightened to resist or make a sound. They got into the trees where it was impossible to see them. The uplands was pure timber country but the foothills also had enough timber to provide shelter. It also provided shade, which made it possible for Roberts to use weapons. Sam and the others had glaring sunlight in their faces.

Roberts took long aim from beside a huge conifer and fired. Sam's running mare folded both front legs and kicked up a cloud of dust where she went down with no knowledge of what had killed her. It was excellent shooting, it also left Sam stunned on the ground. Lynch and the lawman slackened enough for Jake to come up to them. The three riders sat still in hot sunlight looking in the direction of the lethal gunshot. Roberts did not fire again.

Jake said, "If he killed Sam I'll hunt him down wherever he goes," and dismounted. He would have gone to his father-in-law but the other two prevented that.

Lynch was the most reasonable when he said, "We'll get the son of a bitch, Jake. He's on foot."

Roberts watched the three horsemen until Sam Croft arose unsteadily to his feet, looked around and began walking in the wrong direction, eastward away from the man in the timber and away from Lynch, Jake and Constable Wright. The lawman reined his horse to make the interception. He and the others were certain Roberts was watching all this.

Sam Croft had been knocked out of his head by the fall. He was fortunate Roberts had decided to shoot the fastest horse rather than the man on its back.

The constable brought Sam back. He was still so dazed he did not recognise his own son-in-law. There was no shade so they made shade of their saddle animals. As they worked over Sam, Jake occasionally glanced in the direction Roberts had taken his daughter. As moments passed he knew the renegade would be taking Sarah with him on the hike to reach higher ground.

When Sam was beginning to regain awareness Jake left the other three and rode far out and around where that shot had come from before turning north. Common sense told him one fact: He would have to leave the horse behind, large animals moving through forests just naturally made noise.

He rode into shaded timber where there was light but rarely, and only in places where stiff tree tops allowed it to come through, tied the animal and went west until he found feint tracks, one heavy imprint, one rarely visible among the dry, crisp layers of pine and fir needles. There was no grass nor underbush which helped his tracking, but there were also places where he could find no tracks at all and had to quarter like a hunting dog until he found them again.

He had no idea of the time. Only rarely could he see the sun, nor was he interested in time, his entire concentration was on the faint, small tracks and the larger, more obvious ones.

If he'd thought about it he would have been thankful it was Sarah, a hardy child, instead of four-year-old Lottie.

He did not think of anything but following those tracks. If he had been Constable Wright he would have thought differently. This was the best kind of bushwhacking country.

Lynch and the constable took Sam as far as the first tier of trees and left him, fully recovered but badly shaken and with a throbbing headache. He wanted to go with them, they not only refused to allow it but when he would have argued, they told him they would not take much thought to convince Sam that his son-in-law would be in real danger if he found Roberts and

Sarah. Jake was not a manhunter. He wasn't even fast nor accurate with a handgun. Sam agreed to stay, and in fact Lynch and the lawman had not been gone more than a half hour before Sam stretched out and went to sleep, headache and all.

There comes a time in a man's life when, although he thinks he can do everything he once did, he can't. Sam Croft was not only at that age, he was beyond it.

The sun bore down. Among the big old over-ripe pines and firs footsteps were muted, which was helpful if at the same time they weren't easy to follow. At least for a homesteader, a constable and a range-rider.

If it hadn't been for Jake's tracks overlying the other tracks, it was doubtful the constable and Lynch would have done as well as they did. It was this event which allowed the two later trackers to make as good time as they did.

Several times when they encountered

the same rocks Jake had also run across, they had to do as he had done; sashay left and right until they found the sign again.

The day wore along and although heat was not bad among the huge trees as it would be in open country, it was still uncomfortably warm. The forest was also silent. If there had been birds and varmints on the trail, they were no longer there, which, to a seasoned tracker would have told its own tale of earlier trespassers having passed along the trail Jake, Lynch and the constable were travelling with sudden stops and starts in the direction of a camp they had known existed somewhere up in here, but not exactly where.

12

A Dead Man's Ride

JAKE, who was well ahead of his companions, suddenly stopped and swore, something rare for him. When the constable and Lynch came up Jake pointed.

The tracks made an abrupt southerly turn, which was back downhill. Jake made a quick judgement. "He's goin' back where we left the horses."

All three men widened their stride. They had been outsmarted, and their difficulty now was that they had no idea how far ahead Roberts was. If he reached the horses any chance of overtaking him was slight.

Lynch was hurrying when he said, "Sam!" He did not add anything to that. He didn't have to. Roberts would kill Sam Croft if he could. If Sam Croft

176

was in no better shape now as he had been when they left him, he would be a sitting duck for anyone as dangerous and desperate as the renegade was.

They were passing through a thick stand of huge trees when they saw Sarah, exhausted and softly crying. Jake turned aside to hug his daughter. Lynch and the lawman kept going.

Jake wanted Roberts in the worst way. He was torn between remaining with his exhausted daughter and continuing after the man who had done this to her. She clung to him, softly sobbing. When she stopped sobbing and looked up she said, "Catch him, Daddy. He's a terrible man." Her cheek was still slightly red from where Roberts had slapped her. "Get him, Daddy. Go on. I'll rest here for a while then follow on back down out of here."

"You're sure you'll be all right?" he asked.

"Yes. I have to sit here for a while. He dragged me most of the way. He knew you were looking for him . . . Daddy, be careful."

Jake kissed her grimy cheek, looked back once. She waved. He waved back, then doubled his earlier pace to catch up with Lynch and the constable. He was able to accomplish this because it was all downhill.

Lynch looked at him as they hurried. Jake told him Sarah would be all right. Lynch did not look reassured but he said nothing.

As they hastened along Lynch thought Jack Roberts was a fool. He had abandoned the only thing he could have used as a shield. Now, he was on his own, and whether he reached the horses first or not he was much worse off without Sarah than he otherwise would have been. What Lynch thought was that Jack Roberts had to be a high-strung, erratic individual whose desperation had made him rattle-brained. It was a good guess.

The pursuit continued at a swift pace

until the hearts of the pursuers were pounding. They did not slacken their downhill rush.

For Jake nothing now mattered except locating the man who had not only stolen his eldest girl but who had put her through what would have been for any child, days and nights of terror.

The sun was high when Jake, Lynch and Denton Wright saw the thinning of trees ahead. They had made the downhill pursuit in less then half the time they had used reaching the point where Roberts had turned southward.

They slackened pace and veered westward in the direction of the horses. They did not see Sam. They were still using timber-cover. Sam could wait. He'd have to; their objective was the horses.

The horses stood heads up watching something the men could not see until it moved among the speckled shadows of thinner stands of firs and pines. It wasn't just Jack Roberts. He had exchanged one hostage for another. He had Sam Croft, whose hip-holster was empty and had been since the running mare was shot out from under him.

Sam seemed normal. Evidently he had fully recovered. Also, Roberts had found Sam sleeping and had roused him, forced him to accompany Roberts over where the horses were.

Jake, Lynch and the constable halted in shadows near large trees. Roberts kept Sam close. The watching men could distinctly hear Roberts growl a threat at Sam. If it hadn't been for Roberts keeping Sam close to him, his pursuers could have shot him easily. Where they had left the horses there was considerable distance between the trees. There was sunlight in that place. A short distance northward the stand of big trees was more dense. It was back there the men from Coldwater and Jake had first seen movement.

Clearly their flinging pursuit downhill had done as they had hoped; Roberts had not beaten them to the horses by more than minutes. He had Sam shielding him as he untied the roan horse Jake had been riding, after which he flung up the near-side fender to snug up the cinch. His eyes moved constantly.

With only minutes to act Jake suggested a wild, desperate stratagem. He said if the constable and Lynch split up, one heading straight toward Roberts while the other went southward to be in position where Roberts would have to come out into the open, Jake would try to get behind the renegade by circling back uphill and westerly until he could slip back downhill behind Roberts.

His companions gazed at him as though he were simple. Lynch pointed. Roberts was already tightening a cinch. Before Jake's plan could be executed, particularly Jake's part in it, Roberts would be astride with his hostage and moving.

The constable spoke rapidly. "A couple of shots over their heads. Roberts'll duck for cover — if I'm right. Right or wrong it'll spook the horses."

Wright lifted out his six-gun, aimed carefully and fired twice fast. He was correct about one thing, the horses sat back on their shanks, fighting to free themselves. Roberts dropped flat and rolled for shelter. Sam Croft was startled but did not drop, he instead turned to face the shooters which he could only locate by dirty gunsmoke. If the horses had been tied by the reins they would have broken loose. A hemp tie-shank was an altogether different article. Their terror persisted. There was no way for either Sam Croft or Jack Roberts to untie the animals and mount them in their fright.

Roberts called to Sam from behind the base of a large pine. "Get down you old fool! *Get down!*"

Sam got down. He was in plain sight. He made an easy target but Roberts was the target of Jake and the men from Coldwater.

Gradually the dust settled where the

horses came up on their shanks, still shaking and orry-eyed, struggling to break away. They looked steadily in the direction of the fading gunsmoke.

Constable Wright called to the renegade from behind a big tree. "Roberts! Stand up without your weapons!"

The reply came swiftly. "You walk down out into the open where I can see an' shed your weapons — or I'll kill the old man."

Sam Croft, between the hidden renegade and the hidden men who wanted him now had a stand-off so, with no alternative, they reverted to Jake's scheme, but this time while Jake tried to get behind the renegade, Lynch and the constable would try to keep Roberts occupied.

The heat had increased since they had arrived here. Lynch considered his belly-down employer and thought Sam would need water by now.

Constable Wright called again to Roberts. "Don't be a fool, Roberts.

You're not going to ride away from here. We're not the only ones who'll be lookin' for you."

This time there was no reply. The heat bore down, deer flies with a sting almost like a bee, were an annoyance, and while the men in this stand-off had shade, all it did was deflect the sun, it did not mitigate the heat.

Constable Wright tried again. "Roberts! We got your partner. When we're through with him we'll know everything you've had for breakfast for a year."

This time Roberts replied. "He's dead. I seen him go down."

Denton Wright replied tartly. "Wounded, not dead. Not even close to bein' dead."

Sam Croft, flat out in the sun, spoke for the first time. "Lynch? Where's Sarah?"

For also the first time Lynch spoke. "We left her up yonder. We found her Sam. She's worn down but she's all right."

"You left her up there?"

"Sam, she's not much more'n a mile away. She can find her way down to open country. All she's got to do is follow our tracks."

Sam was silent; Lynch hadn't completely reassured him but for the moment there was nothing he could do.

Roberts called again. "Tell you what, Constable. You fellers let me take one of the horses and leave, or I'll shoot the old man."

Lynch looked at the constable, who returned the look. Neither man doubted that Roberts would do it even though he would be losing his only bargaining chip if he shot Sam Croft. Without Sam he would not be able to even reach the horses. Lynch's opinion of Jack Roberts dropped another few notches.

He called back before the lawman could. "If you shoot Mister Croft, you'll lose your hostage. When you do that we'll take you as sure as hell's hot. There won't be nothin' to stop us."

The silence settled again. If Roberts thought Lynch had been right, he had to at least begin to understand how desperate his situation was. The trouble here was that Lynch was not convinced the renegade would understand. He was in a bad spot, knew that for a fact, and was likely to reach for any way to get out of it, without using reason. His kind reasoned through the barrel of a gun.

Sam seemed completely recovered, he remained close to Roberts and watched everything Roberts did. In fact it seemed to the men from Coldwater and Jake that he stayed too close. Otherwise they might have risked a shot.

Roberts fumbled with the latigo, tugged it once until the latigo overlapped. He swore because he had to free the overlap before he could make the cinch tighter. Flighty people are commonly high-strung. Roberts worked fast freeing the overlap to take another pull on the cinch. As he worked Sam Croft

186

watched. Jake, who knew his father-in-law better than his companions did, was close to getting around behind the renegade. He was close enough to see Sam's face. Sam's eyes were slits, not the result of sunlight. His jaw was set like stone.

When Roberts was ready to mount he drew his Colt, aimed it at Sam and told him to mount behind the cantle, then swung up and kicked his foot free of the left stirrup. In the brief moment required for Sam to mount Roberts was a sitting target, but Sam used the empty stirrup, swung up behind the renegade and the only decent opportunity the men on the ground had to shoot passed in seconds.

Roberts had protected his back. He did not warm the horse out but savagely hooked it with both spurs. The startled animal jumped out and lit down running hard.

Jake had been close enough to shoot before his father-in-law mounted behind Roberts. He hadn't fired because Sam was too close. Also, he knew his accuracy with handguns was bad, but he had been waiting for Sam to be out of the way and had taken a hand rest across the low limb of a tree. After Roberts jumped out the horse he had to stand and watch. None of them could shoot with Sam Croft behind the saddle. They ran for their horses. In this kind of heat a horse carrying double its normal weight, even the toughest animal could not reach its maximum speed nor last long if forced to continue running.

Jake flung into the saddle of Lynch's horse. Constable Wright his own horse. They left Lynch behind, watching.

Roberts' pursuers did not gain for several hundred yards, then they began to gain slowly but steadily. They never caught Roberts, and what happened made them haul back.

Abruptly, both the renegade and Sam Croft went off the horse locked together. The horse continued to run for a quarter mile, before it stopped and looked back at the struggling men on the ground.

Jake was slightly ahead of the lawman riding in a slow lope. Sam had deliberately put his arms around the renegade as most people did when riding double. He had suddenly hurled all his weight to the left. Unsuspecting Jack Roberts had no time to grab the saddle horn. It wouldn't have done much good if he had, Sam Croft's weight did the rest.

Where they landed the drying summertime grass had been cropped close. Dust flew when the men locked together struck hard. Sam struck hard on his right side, his grip gave way. He had broken his arm but that would not be noted until later.

Roberts struggled to his feet, aimed a furious kick, missed and leaned, hoisted Sam to his feet and swung a wide haymaker, which Sam saw coming and twisted sideways. He took the blow on a slant. It was enough contact to make Sam stumble.

An enraged Jack Roberts sprang at Sam, who fended off another strike with his left arm, but not the next two blows which drove Sam to his knees.

Jake was almost abreast of the downed riders before he drew and cocked his six-gun. Constable Wright was about five yards behind. He saw Jake draw his sidearm and reined back a little.

Jake rode up to within twenty feet of the enraged renegade, reined to a stop, called to Roberts who, in his present insanely furious frame of mind, may not have heard. Roberts stepped back to aim a kick at Sam Croft's head when Jake leaned and pulled the trigger.

The poorest gunman on earth could not miss Roberts at that distance, and Jake was not the poorest, just one of the poorest.

The bullet hit Jack Roberts through the lights. Its force at that range hurled him across Sam, who was dazed and in considerable pain but who one-handedly pushed Roberts clear and got to his feet, looking first at the dead renegade, then at his son-in-law who cocked his six-gun for another shot, held it aimed until he saw the blood, then let the hammer down and holstered the weapon.

Sam eased down on the ground holding his right arm and gritting his teeth. The pain was excruciating. All that struggling after it had been broken made the pain worse than it otherwise might have been. Sam was sweating rivulets as Jake and Denton Wright dismounted, rolled Roberts on his back, saw the sightless eyes and bloody chest, from which no blood was flowing. The lawman retrieved Robert's hat, dropped it over his face.

They went over to Sam Croft, who spoke through gritted teeth. "Arm's broke. I'd give ten dollars for some brandy right now."

The constable went after the loose horse which, fortunately, was easily caught. As he was leading the horse back Lynch Miller was walking toward them from the opposite direction.

When Lynch arrived Jake had fashioned a sling from two bandanas knotted together. He helped his father-in-law to his feet and steadied him. Sam was too old for this sort of thing; if he hadn't recognised that before, he did now as he said, "Damned foolish thing to do, wasn't it?"

Jake shook his head. "It was the only way, Sam."

The older man gazed at his son-in-law. "I didn't know you could shoot that good."

"I can't. I aimed at his head."

Sam made a strained smile. "You saved my bacon, Jake. I owe you."

Lynch and the constable arrived. Lynch made a clucking sound and shook his head. Sam blew out a ragged breath before he said, "Lynch, I didn't see no other way."

"They'd of overtaken him, Sam. You could've busted your back."

Constable Wright was within hearing distance. "I think he did exactly right."

Lynch let the topic drop. He would have done the same thing if their situations had been reversed — if he had thought of it.

They were tying the corpse behind the lawman's cantle when Jake looked back. Sarah was standing solemnly in a clearing watching everything they did. Jake rode back, hoisted her behind the cantle. She did not speak; she had just seen her first killing.

They struck out on a southeasterly course, which was the course to Coldwater. There was not much conversation. Sam Croft was white as a flour sack. Every step of his mount jarred. Lynch thought it had been a clean break, in which case someone with experience in Coldwater could set the bone. No one else even made a guess.

The sun was lowering and its colour was changing from dazzling yellow to a variety of copper tan. The heat was steady and unchanging but by the time they had town in sight shadows were forming. They did not, however, touch the area of the riders until they reached the unkempt big tree. Jake rode over, plucked the folded wad of greenbacks he had jammed into the tree-crotch. pocketed the money and rejoined the others. He did not offer the money to Sam who was in no condition to reach for it and probably right at this time could not have cared less about money.

A few lamps had been lighted although dusk had not fully settled. The roadway was almost completely deserted as tired people on tired — and thirsty — horses plodded as far as the preacher's residence, dismounted wearily and were met at the door by Anna, the others were at supper. She took one look at her husband, threw an arm around him, led him to a sofa in the parlour, made him lie down, then fled to the kitchen to announce the arrival of Jake, Lynch, the constable, her husband — and Sarah.

13

The Last Dead Man

THE one person in Coldwater who had set bones, cured spavins on horses and even upon the occasions when he was permitted, acted as midwife, was the local wood worker, Core Pendelton, a large, fair-haired man with the gift of many talents which he used satisfactorily when he was sober. He was not a constant drinker. He might go several months without going near the saloon, but when he did go up there, he invariably went on a drunk for several days straight running, and usually was sick as a dog for several days afterwards.

It was during one of his "dry" periods that Reverend Caldwell found him making coffins, which he stacked against one wall of his shop, something he did in his spare time.

He returned to the preacher's residence with the reverend, examined Sam Croft and pronounced his diagnosis as a clean break six or eight inches below the elbow. He asked if Reverend Caldwell had any laudanum, which the preacher did not have before explaining to Sam without laudanum when he pulled the bone-ends so that they meshed and could be set, the pain was likely to be very bad.

Sam listened, nodded and said, "Just fix it."

The large man groped until he located the precise break, told Sam to grit his teeth, took both the upper and lower arms in powerful hands and jerked.

Sam fainted.

With Anna and others watching, Pendelton then set about wrapping the arm firmly after which he made a sling of one of Fannie Caldwell's kitchen towels, gave the unconscious old cowman a gentle pat on the shoulder as he said, "That's even better'n laudanum. You won't feel drug out when you wake up."

He arose as Lynch fished forth some crumpled greenbacks. The large man selected one bill, nodded around and left the house.

Sam did not regain consciousness for another ten minutes, and when he did there was sweat on his face and pain in his eyes. He asked Anna what had happened. When she told him Sam raised up enough to see his bandaged arm in its sling, and sank back looking at the preacher as he asked if there was any whiskey in the house. Reverend Caldwell neither nodded nor spoke. He went into the kitchen, reached as high as he could for a bottle on a top cupboard shelf, took the bottle back into the parlour and offered it to Sam. It wasn't whiskey it was brandy.

Sam took two swallows, handed back the bottle, screwed up his face and blew out a flammable breath. The brandy worked fast. He looked up at the preacher and said, "What was that?"

"Brandy."

"It burns, don't it?"

The minister answered predictably. "I don't know. I've never tasted it. I found it on the doorstep one morning after I'd officiated at the funeral of the man who used to own the saloon."

Sam's mind had already passed to another topic. He addressed his wife. "Sarah . . . ?"

"She's fine, except for some problems. She saw her father kill a man. We bathed and fed her. She fell asleep at the dinner table so we put her to bed. The other children wanted to see her. We told them they could when she awakened, that she was exhausted."

Anna fell briefly silent, then spoke again looking directly at her husband. "Do you remember what happened, Sam?"

"I yanked that — man — off the horse. He fell atop me an' broke my arm."

"I meant do you know how that man was killed."

"Jake shot him."

Anna nodded, turned and left the room, which was just as well, in Sam Croft's condition the brandy worked as it often did on worn-down people. He fell asleep.

The constable arrived at the preacher's house in mid-morning with an odd tale. The late morning coach southbound for Coldwater had found an unconscious man who had been shot sprawled at roadside beneath that solitary big old tree several miles northward. The coach was carrying three drummers and an old woman with a mouth like a bear trap. The whip halted, got down to examine what he assumed was a corpse. He and the three male passengers were startled when Coombs opened his eyes.

They got him into the coach looking like he'd been butchering hogs. The wizened old woman the others expected to probably faint or protest put a gimlet gaze on Coombs and said, "Well, I expect you asked for it. I know your kind," and did not look at the bloody renegade nor say another word all the way to Coldwater.

Coombs was now at the jailhouse, weaker than a kitten but bandaged as best Core Pendleton could do, washed, fed, and given a dram of laced coffee. When the constable had left to come up to the preacher's house, Coombs was sleeping like the dead.

There was more, which the constable did not mention because he knew nothing about it. Townsmen had taken Jack Roberts from behind the saddle where they had found him, carried him down to Core Pendleton's wood-working shop, placed an empty coffin across two saw-horses. When Pendleton returned to his shop he got a shock. There was a greying, bloody dead man where there had not been one before. Roberts looked terrible.

Pendleton placed a lid over the coffin and headed for the saloon.

The townspeople knew Sarah had

been brought back. They had to guess about Roberts, in whom they were less interested than they were in the live renegade at the jailhouse. There was nothing they could do by way of punishment for the dead man but there was something they could do with Coombs, which they discussed at great length, not only at the saloon but also in just about every other business establishment in town, and they intended to do it.

Constable Wright was still at the preacher's house when Sam awakened feeling better; at least his broken arm was no longer particularly painful although it was swollen almost twice its normal size and throbbed beneath the tight bandage.

He, Jake and Sam talked in the parlour until Lynch returned from the cafe to announce a lynch-mob was forming down at the general store.

Denton Wright left immediately. He was not against hanging Coombs but he was against mob-lynching. He had seen how crudely lynchings ordinarily were. Sometimes the knot was not tied correctly and victims strangled in mid-air while doing gruesome gyrations which were sickening to watch.

When he reached the general store the place was crowded. Mostly with men but also a sprinkling of irate women. He stopped in the doorway blocking an exit. The crowd became silent when it saw him. He slowly shook his head before saying, "We'll hang him but it'll be done right. Go on home. You'll know when it's time."

One man protested. "Dent, he got everyone involved. What he done deserves a rope."

The lawman replied to that remark calmly. "He'll get it. But not by a mob. Go on home."

"Why not do it now," the same man asked, "and get it over with?"

"For one thing he's sick. For another thing you'd likely have to carry him out of town to hang him. He lost a lot of blood. You wouldn't want to carry him out there and have to prop him up. Finally, I've seen lynch-mob-hangings. They're usually done bad. The victims don't get their necks broke, they flip'n flop in the air until they strangle to death. Take my word for it, it'll haunt you as long as you live."

The crowd was silent until a woman asked when it would be done. Constable Wright nodded in her direction. "As soon as he can stand on his own feet. Now go home, an' don't some of you get the notion you can do it on your own."

The crowd trickled out of the store, silent and sullen. After they were gone the storekeeper addressed Constable Wright. "Did you get their money, Dent?"

Constable Wright's patience had been worn thin. He gave a sharp answer. "Where would they spend it in a mountain hideout? Yes; the dead one had it in his pockets an' the other one had it in a belt around his middle. The money Mister Croft give Jake was stuck in a crotch of that big tree beside the road north of town. We got it all. In a day or two when things settle down I'll see that everyone who chipped in will get their money back." He paused, looking at the storekeeper. "Who got 'em to meet in your store?"

The merchant's gaze drifted away, colour came into his cheeks. He was so slow to answer the constable spoke first. "Don't do it again," and walked out of the store.

Over at the jailhouse he went down into his cell room, stopped in front of Coombs' cell and gazed at the man on the wall-bunk. Coombs said, "You got any whiskey?"

Denton Wright returned to his office without answering, rummaged in a wooden box and returned with a half-full bottle. He entered the cell and held the bottle just long enough for Coombs to swallow twice then straightened up with the bottle.

The renegade said, "Hell, a couple of swallows won't help."

The constable replied shortly. "It's all you get. How do you feel?"

"Like I been drug through a knothole . . . What's your name?"

"Denton Wright. Why?"

"How did I get here?"

"They found you under a big tree north of town when the southbound morning stage come along." Wright stood silent for a moment before he also said, "You're lucky that feller didn't kill you."

Coombs looked sardonically upward. "I don't feel lucky."

Wright did not reply, he relocked the door and returned to his office. For a fact the damned fool wasn't lucky.

It was a hot day. He was relaxing when the liveryman walked in. Some rangemen had found a loose, saddled horse and had brought him in to him at the barn. He thought it might have belonged to the renegade in the jailhouse. The liveryman had gone through the saddlebags and put what he had found on the lawman's desk.

It was two crumpled wanted dodgers, both for Dan Coombs, one from Nevada, the other from Texas. Both places wanted Coombs for murder.

Constable Wright sighed, put the dodgers aside and took the liveryman up to the saloon for something wet and bracing.

The saloon's proprietor had been among the mob at the general store. He served both customers, kept an expressionless look on his face and barely spoke.

The burly liveryman watched the saloonman walk away. He was perplexed. "What's eatin' him?"

Denton Wright explained about the mob at the general store. The liveryman downed his jolt of popskull before saying, "I heard about it."

"I didn't see you there," stated Wright.

The liveryman blew out a fiery breath before speaking again. "I wasn't there. I was told about the meetin', but I'm not strong on lynchings.

My brother was lynched back in Missouri. I'll never as long as I live forget how he looked when I cut him down."

The reasonable thing for the constable to do was ask why the liveryman's brother had been lynched. He didn't ask but when they returned to the roadway the burly, bearded man said, "For stealin' one horse, an' not much of a horse at that."

The constable went up to Reverend Caldwell's house. There was a distinct scent of cooking. Until he smelled it he hadn't been aware that it was dinnertime.

There were four men in the parlour. Sam Croft sitting up, Jake his son-in-law, the preacher and Lynch Miller. Whatever they had been discussing ended with the arrival of the lawman.

Lynch asked if the lynch-mob was still at the store. Dent Wright shook his head as he headed for a chair. "No. They all went home." He added nothing to this.

A brief silence ensued before Sam Croft broke it. "What happened to the money, Constable?"

"I got it. All but the money Jake took from the tree. When things settle down I'll see that folks get it back . . . How do you feel?"

"Worse than I felt yesterday," Sam replied, and asked a question of his own. "How does that bastard in your jailhouse feel?"

"Not too good. He lost considerable blood."

"What're you goin' to do with him?"

"Hang him as soon as he's strong enough to walk."

There was a lapse of silence before Sam said, "You got any ideas about how I can repay the folks in Coldwater for helping?"

The constable was quiet for several moments before he answered. "Just tell 'em thanks . . . They're good people."

Sam spoke in his characteristic fashion, straightforward and blunt. "I'll thank 'em, but what they done deserves more'n just bein' thanked. What does the town need?"

The constable considered the hat he was holding between his knees before he matched Croft's bluntness with some of his own. "They need a schoolhouse. Right now the lady who's teachin' them is doin' it in her house."

Sam asked another, practical, question. "You got a place to put it?"

"Yes. Several places. Folk's planned about it a long time."

"You got any idea what it'll cost?"

"The feller who bandaged you, Core Pendleton, figured out what it would cost last year. Three hundred dollars. We got jars at the general store and the saloon, but contributions don't add up very fast."

Sam's next remark was also straightforward. "If I give you three hundred dollars will you put it in the jar at the store?"

The constable stopped turning his hat. "Yes," he said, and again there was a moment of silence. It was broken by the constable. "Mister Croft you don't have to do that. Folks was glad to help."

"An' I want to be glad too," Sam replied. He fumbled with a shirt pocket, withdrew a thick packet of bills, counted out the money and handed it to the lawman. The constable sat a moment then arose. "We could name the schoolhouse for you," he said, and Croft shook his head. "Coldwater School District sounds better."

He saw Lynch nod slightly.

Constable Wright left shortly before Anna called the men to dinner. She hadn't heard what had transpired in the parlour until Lynch told her. She beamed at her husband. Later she would reward him better.

That evening a fresher-looking Sarah joined the others for supper. She approached her father from behind his chair, leaned and gave him a strong hug, then went silently to her chair.

Two days later Denton Wright told Sam his prisoner wasn't improving, he seemed to be getting worse. He went in search of Core Pendleton, but his look of horror at the bloody, filthy dead man in the coffin at his shop had sent him off on one of his period drunks. He was dead to the world in the backroom of the shop. The smell of whiskey in the little room was strong enough to require only a brief visit in order for an accurate diagnosis of his ailment to be made. The constable went up to the preacher's house.

He was worried. Jake, Sam Croft and Lynch went back to the jailhouse with the constable. Sam Croft recognised the symptoms instantly and dryly said, "If you figure to hang him, you better not put it off. He's got blood poisoning."

Sam Croft had no reason to say anything around town and the constable said nothing either, but somehow as days passed and the constable diverted questions concerning the hanging, the rumour speculation concerning his illness, even the actual condition was touched upon, but wasn't given much creditability. There were other more probable likelihoods. More colourful and common.

Time passed and Coombs became less lucid. He had a high fever and during his lucid periods drank inordinately large amounts of water, which appeared to do nothing for the fever although it increased his sweating.

Reverend Caldwell went once to look at him, and shook his head. He had little knowledge of things physical except that after all his years as a minister, death and buryings, he knew the look of impending death. He didn't mention the local anticipation of hanging, he simply said. "May God have mercy on his soul."

It was one of those things that would eventually become common knowledge and the more dogged townsmen, with excellent hindsight, blamed the constable for not allowing them to hang Coombs earlier, evidently overlooking the fact that earlier he had been too weak to stand. Otherwise the fact that there would now be no hanging, folks accepted as fact. Some were uneasy about Coombs dying. The most reflective among them saw every death as a harbinger of their own mortality and did the only thing they could do, they waited.

Coombs was tough. He had never been anything else. He lingered. As days passed local interest lost its vindictiveness. Denton Wright was asked daily how Coombs was faring, and the constable answered honestly that although he would surely die he was taking a long time to do it.

But eventually he died. It happened in the night. When the constable got down to the jailhouse the following morning his prisoner was cool to the touch and beginning to stiffen.

He took the corpse down the back alley unseen until he crossed Main Street to reach the coffin-maker's shop where Core Pendleton had been sober and at work again for three days.

This time, since he had known as had everyone else the renegade was dying, he was not shocked. He had been unable to march to the graveyard when townspeople hauled Jack Roberts out there in an old buckboard, but this time he and the constable put Coombs in a wooden box, which was on trestles and this time Core nailed down the lid. Wright went to the livery barn, engaged the same buckboard, and when they loaded Coombs' coffin Lynch drove to one of the previously prepared holes in the ground. Two men from the saloon rode along to close the grave afterwards.

As with Roberts the cemetery had only those mourners, and they weren't really mourners, particularly the men from the saloon who would shovel in the dirt.

Reverend Caldwell gave a very short eulogy, read from the Bible briefly, and stood watching as Coombs went into the ground. There was no discreet period of waiting for mourners to leave. The saloon hangers-on who ordinarily made an extra dollar digging and closing graves and were usually disinterested in who was buried, pushed forward and immediately went to work shoveling. It was getting hot. They wanted to get back to the pleasant coolness of the saloon.

Sam Croft paid them; instead of thanking Sam they took the money, nodded and went back to their work.

They said they'd walk back, the others could return without them. They had the best reason in the world for this; they had brought a pony of whiskey to the graveyard with them.

On the ride back very little was said because, although some townsfolk would feel cheated, watching someone being buried even someone like Dan Coombs, was a time for each person to turn inward.

They returned the wagon, Constable Wright went to disinfect Coombs' empty cell, then sit in his office as solemn as an owl, while Jake,

Sam Croft, Lynch and the preacher returned to the parson's house where the women kept quiet but Jake's children ran to him all talking at once. It would be many years before they would understand their father's silent solicitude on this day.

14

Frank Talk

JAKE got his wagon and team from the liveryman, drove up to the preacher's house and parked. Its contents had been rummaged but as far as Jake could see nothing had been taken.

Sam did an uncharacteristic thing; knowing the preacher would not accept money for all he and his wife had done, Sam put a fifty dollar green back in his Bible while the others were loading the wagon. The preacher's daughter and Sarah embraced. They had grown fond of each other. Each girl promised to write and they were teary-eyed at the parting.

Anna and Fannie were also teary-eyed as they hugged each other. Lynch worked at the loading without words, but when he and the reverend shook hands the minister also gave Lynch a rough pat on the back. Neither man was particularly demonstrative.

It was a pleasant morning. There would be heat later but as they left Coldwater with miles to cover, everyone waving, visibility was perfect, as was the day.

Sam asked Jake to ride the roan horse he had purchased and let him drive the wagon. He and Anna sat side by side on the wagon-seat, both quiet, pensively so until Coldwater was no longer in sight.

Jake hadn't thought it odd for Sam to want to ride with Anna.

The children were under the makeshift texas Jake had improvised, cool, happy to be on their way home, and boisterous for a while before they settled down. The boys teased Sarah. Lottie fell asleep holding her rag doll. The heat built up before the wagon reached timber country where there was shade for miles, and pine-sap fragrance.

Several times since leaving Coldwater Sam glanced at Anna. She was sitting relaxed, hands in her lap looking thoughtfully straight ahead.

When they stopped near a watercourse slightly after midday and Sam helped water the team with Jake, Anna watched him working with one arm and almost smiled. Sam had always been an individual who pitched in, even when he didn't have to.

Jake started a conversation by complimenting Sam on the quality of the running-horse he had ridden to Coldwater. Sam answered as casually as Jake had spoken, almost as though they were longtime friends.

"It was a good animal. Usually them part thoroughbreds don't have bottom, but that one sure did. I pushed a little harder than I might have. That horse never sulked nor dragged a foot." Sam was kneeling to fill a bucket for the team when he said, "About havin' your wife taken to town for a decent burial . . . "

Jake stood perfectly still holding his bucketful of water looking down where Sam was kneeling. "She wanted to be buried on the ranch."

Sam struggled to his feet without picking up his full bucket. "And she told you that?"

"They were almost her last words."

Anna could hear and see them both. Her husband looked from Jake to the little creek as he said, "I didn't know . . . We'll have her brought — home. Where did she want to be buried — did she say?"

"No. Just that she wanted to be buried on the ranch."

Sam continued gazing at the creek. After a moment he said, "Let's ask her mother. She'd know."

Sam was right. Anna remembered a little knoll not far from the ranch and Jake's homestead. From the top she could see both places. They listened, and both men brightened. "That'll be the place," Sam said.

Later in the day while Jake and

Lynch marvelled at Sam's ability to handle the lines one-handed, which wasn't difficult at all to a man who had, for one reason or another, driven teams with one hand before, Joseph asked Lynch if he could ride the mare tied to the tailgate, the animal Anna had ridden to Coldwater.

Lynch told the lad to ask his grandmother. When she smiled and nodded Lynch untied the shank, boosted Joseph to the saddle and rode beside him in silence. He knew this wasn't finished; he and Sam Croft would talk, either before they got home or afterward.

When Lottie awakened Jake took her behind his saddle. She was happy and laughed a lot. Sarah was quiet. Jake noticed and asked her if she felt all right. She nodded. "I'm thirsty, is all."

Jake rode close to the tailgate to hand her his canteen, and remained there until she handed it back. Looking solemnly at her father she said, "I love you daddy."

Sam and Anna rarely spoke. Sam because he was afraid to and Anna because she didn't believe it was necessary. Sam eventually broke the long silence between them when evening arrived and everyone piled out to make camp. He followed her to the creek with dust descending to lend them both a shadowy look of their long-departed youth. Anna turned and smiled. Sam was encouraged enough to say, "Anna . . . That talk of leaving me . . . "

"I can't apologise for it, Sam," she replied quietly. "I was furious with you."

He was expressionless as he said, "Then you figure to do it?"

Her smile lingered and softened. "No. We'll bring Susan home. In Coldwater you acted — human — Sam. You surprised me. Over the years I've rarely seen you act that way."

Sam continued to look grave when he replied to her. "I gave it some thought, Anna. With one arm I'll have trouble. Anyway, it's getting harder for me to roll out of bed lately . . . I'm old Anna. Maybe we don't have much time any more . . . Lynch is the best man I can think of to mind the ranch if we travel a little."

"Sam, I'd like to go to Texas. I have kin there I haven't seen since we've been married, and you're right about Lynch. He's not fond of you, Sam, but if there ever was a man loyal to his brand it's Lynch Miller."

Sam said, "And Jake?"

"He saved your life, Sam. He's always tried to be your friend and neighbour."

Sam conceded the first point if not the second. "For a fact he saved my bacon, Anna. A man can't ever forget something like that."

"It's more'n just that, Sam. Susan loved him. His children love him . . . I love him, Sam. He's a good man, he's never crossed you an' you went out of your way to show your disapproval of his marriage to your daughter. Own up, Sam. He's your kin."

Sam was intrigued; Anna had never spoken like this to him in all their married years. He was wearing a hint of an admiring little smile when he said, "Anna, I never knew there was two sides to you."

He opened his wary arms to her. She hesitated, then went into his embrace. While he was holding her he said, "You think Lynch can handle things?"

"Sam, he's been with us almost seven years. He knows as much about the ranch as you do. Of course he can."

"Then let's go to Texas, Anna."

She hugged him hard.

THE END

BRETT RANDALL, GAMBLER
E. B. Mann

Larry Day had the choice of running away from the law or of assuming a dead man's place. No matter what he decided he was bound to end up dead.

THE GUNSHARP
William R. Cox

The Eggerleys weren't very smart. They trained their sights on Will Carney and Arizona's biggest blood bath began.

THE DEPUTY OF SAN RIANO
Lawrence A. Keating and
Al. P. Nelson

When a man fell dead from his horse, Ed Grant was spotted riding away from the scene. The deputy sheriff rode out after him and came up against everything from gunfire to dynamite.

FARGO: MASSACRE RIVER
John Benteen

The ambushers up ahead had now blocked the road. Fargo's convoy was a jumble, a perfect target for the insurgents' weapons!

SUNDANCE: DEATH IN THE LAVA
John Benteen

The Modoc's captured the wagon train and its cargo of gold. But now the halfbreed they called Sundance was going after it . . .

HARSH RECKONING
Phil Ketchum

Five years of keeping himself alive in a brutal prison had made Brand tough and careless about who he gunned down . . .

SUNDANCE: SILENT ENEMY
John Benteen

A lone crazed Cheyenne was on a personal war path. They needed to pit one man against one crazed Indian. That man was Sundance.

LASSITER
Jack Slade

Lassiter wasn't the kind of man to listen to reason. Cross him once and he'll hold a grudge for years to come — if he let you live that long.

LAST STAGE TO GOMORRAH
Barry Cord

Jeff Carter, tough ex-riverboat gambler, now had himself a horse ranch that kept him free from gunfights and card games. Until Sturvesant of Wells Fargo showed up.

McALLISTER ON THE COMANCHE CROSSING
Matt Chisholm

The Comanche, McAllister owes them a life — and the trail is soaked with the blood of the men who had tried to outrun them before.

QUICK-TRIGGER COUNTRY
Clem Colt

Turkey Red hooked up with Curly Bill Graham's outlaw crew. But wholesale murder was out of Turk's line, so when range war flared he bucked the whole border gang alone . . .

CAMPAIGNING
Jim Miller

Ambushed on the Santa Fe trail, Sean Callahan is saved by two Indian strangers. But there'll be more lead and arrows flying before the band join Kit Carson against the Comanches.

FIGHTING RAMROD
Charles N. Heckelmann

Most men would have cut their losses, but Frazer counted the bullets in his guns and said he'd soak the range in blood before he'd give up another inch of what was his.

LONE GUN
Eric Allen

Smoke Blackbird had been away too long. The Lequires had seized the Blackbird farm, forcing the Indians and settlers off, and no one seemed willing to fight! He had to fight alone.

THE THIRD RIDER
Barry Cord

Mel Rawlins wasn't going to let anything stand in his way. His father was murdered, his two brothers gone. Now Mel rode for vengeance.

GUNSLINGER'S RANGE
Jackson Cole

Three escaped convicts are out for revenge. They won't rest until they put a bullet through the head of the dirty snake who locked them behind bars.

RUSTLER'S TRAIL
Lee Floren

Jim Carlin knew he would have to stand up and fight because he had staked his claim right in the middle of Big Ike Outland's best grass.

THE TRUTH ABOUT SNAKE RIDGE
Marshall Grover

The troubleshooters came to San Cristobal to help the needy. For Larry and Stretch the turmoil began with a brawl and then an ambush.

HELL RIDERS
Steve Mensing

Wade Walker's kid brother, Duane, was locked up in the Silver City jail facing a rope at dawn. Wade was a ruthless outlaw, but he was smart, and he had vowed to have his brother out of jail before morning!

DESERT OF THE DAMNED
Nelson Nye

The law was after him for the murder of a marshal — a murder he didn't commit. Breen was after him for revenge — and Breen wouldn't stop at anything . . . blackmail, a frameup . . . or murder.

DAY OF THE COMANCHEROS
Steven C. Lawrence

Their very name struck terror into men's hearts — the Comancheros, a savage army of cutthroats who swept across Texas, leaving behind a bloodstained trail of robbery and murder.

ARIZONA DRIFTERS
W. C. Tuttle

When drifting Dutton and Lonnie Steelman decide to become partners they find that they have a common enemy in the formidable Thurston brothers.

TOMBSTONE
Matt Braun

Wells Fargo paid Luke Starbuck to outgun the silver-thieving stagecoach gang at Tombstone. Before long Luke can see the only thing bearing fruit in this eldorado will be the gallows tree.

HIGH BORDER RIDERS
Lee Floren

Buckshot McKee and Tortilla Joe cut the trail of a border tough who was running Mexican beef into Texas. They stopped the smuggler in his tracks.

FARGO: PANAMA GOLD
John Benteen

With foreign money behind him, Buckner was going to destroy the Panama Canal before it could be completed. Fargo's job was to stop Buckner.

FARGO:
THE SHARPSHOOTERS
John Benteen

The Canfield clan, thirty strong were raising hell in Texas. Fargo was tough enough to hold his own against the whole clan.

PISTOL LAW
Paul Evan Lehman

Lance Jones came back to Mustang for just one thing — revenge! Revenge on the people who had him thrown in jail.